MACMILLAN CARIBBEAN WRITERS

The Festival of San Joaquin

Zee Edgell

MACMILLAN
CARIBBEAN

Macmillan Education
4 Crinan Street, London N1 9XW
A division of Macmillan Publishers Limited
Companies and representatives throughout the world

www.macmillan-caribbean.com

ISBN: 978-0-230-02991-0

First published by Heinemann Publishers Limited, 1997
This edition published 2008

Typeset by EXPO Holdings
Cover design and illustration by Tim Gravestock

Printed and bound in China

2020 2019 2018 2017 2016
10 9 8 7 6 5 4 3 2

To Al, Holly, Randall and my parents,
with love and thanks

Part 1

I am out of gaol now. In a certain sad and terrible way I sometimes feel that it is the second time I have been released. There is no one to meet me. I did not expect anyone. I do not know if I have anyone left. I had three children before I went into prison on March 20, another Monday in 1989, nearly fifteen months ago. It seems like an eternity.

The railings and the grillework of the courthouse steps are blindingly white in the sunlight. They make my eyes flood with water, and I remove dark glasses from my bag and put them on. I feel a bit safer now; the light seems more remote. The red flowers on the flamboyant trees in the park across the street are muted. The trembling in my body lessens and I can move again. My fingers are icy cold.

The lawyer, Mr Reuben Oliver, his teeth bright against the blue-black of his skin, is smiling at me, expecting a change of plan, perhaps, or a smile of thank you. I wait as he mops the sweat from his forehead, and I watch as he transfers his black robes from one plump arm to the other.

"We did very well, Luz Marina, under the circumstances. Three years' probation seems long but the time will soon pass. How are you feeling? Belize City can be a miserable place in June." He puts his free hand under my elbow to guide me down the steps.

Incapable of speech, I smile, and feel myself veering to the left, away from his touch. But because I am smiling, he seems pleased, and smiles even more widely, a smile of victory. I hang my head. Hair shields my face and eyes. I do not feel triumphant.

1

However, I must have done the right thing for a photographer on the sidewalk is smiling too. Perhaps our photographs will appear in the newspapers again this weekend. For the last time, please God. It is nearly noon and soon the radio stations will be broadcasting the verdict to the country. In San Joaquín, my home, seventy-two miles away, everyone will be listening; about that I feel certain.

I never wanted to raise my hand against Salvador Joaquín. I never wanted to lose my children, or to stand exposed like this to the public gaze. Having to do these things killed something inside me, and now I am someone I don't want to be.

I used to be able to do the right thing nearly always, but that too seems like a long time ago. I worked hard in Doña Catalina's household, and wanted to marry Salvador, her son, as my family hoped I would. Nowadays, I always say "it seems" because I am wondering whether I have lost my sense of time, or maybe I mean my sense of where, if any place, I fit in.

I do know that I am now in the habit of talking to myself, instructing myself, cautioning myself, so much more than I remember doing before. I also know that, in certain areas, I feel free, freed, at liberty, for the first time in my life it seems. At some other time, I must have felt free; I must have had the freedom of choice. The truth is that I regularly shy away from the sad and painful memories of that time. The doctor has urged me to think about those days, to speak with her about them, but so far I cannot. Perhaps I will find the strength to do so, some day.

We have reached the sidewalk and I try not to look towards the people lining the streets, murmuring as I walk by. I turn instead to look at the vendors outside the gates of Scots Kirk, selling fruits, vegetables and flowers. I look at an old *señor*, selling purple orchids in brown coconut husks, who is pretending that he does not see me. His straight grey hair, and the wrinkles in his sunburnt face, remind me of my father. Before his injury, Papá

Apolonio used to wear the same kind of straw hat, the front skinned back whenever he worked in the *milpa*.

"Wait here in the shade, Luz Marina, while I fetch the car," Mr Oliver is saying. I nod, watching him walk towards the dozens of vehicles parked near the sea-wall.

It is a relief to reach the foreshore, to the rear of the courthouse. Here I can no longer see the flowers.

In preparation for our wedding, Salvador and his friends mixed pink, red and yellow flowers from the frangipani trees, ixora bushes and alamanda vines that grow everywhere. They had a spree that afternoon, drinking beer as they walked from my family's hut on the *milpa*, to the banks of the Río Caracol, where they emptied buckets of bruised and wilting petals into a large dory, loaned to them by a fisherman.

Mamá Sofía, and my sisters Perla and Concha, had embroidered a bedspread as our wedding gift. This, everyone decided, should be placed over the petals so that I would not soil my dress. Although I would have preferred to go to church in Salvador's car, I was moved by his attempt to include me in his family's traditions. I put my arms around his neck, and kissed his lips, thin, wide, and warm.

Everyone clapped and, from the doorway of our hut in the distance, Papá Apolonio cheered. I watched the setting sun shining on Salvador's black hair, which tapered to a point at the back of his neck. Over six feet tall, Salvador was handsome and slender then. He dressed elegantly, especially for dinner at his mother's house. On those evenings he wore white, long-sleeved *guayabreras*, with gold cufflinks, dark trousers and black patent leather shoes.

Later on in life, I discovered that it was only one of Salvador's stories; his family had no such tradition. But that was Salvador all over. He had elaborate visions and ideas about his family and about himself. However, he didn't stay interested in many things for very long; and he always seemed to want the exact person, or thing, he couldn't have.

That afternoon, as we were about to leave, I looked again towards the river, crying out before I could stop myself, "Over there, Salva, look. The bamboo is in flower!"

His grey eyes darkened as he glanced briefly into the bushes on the opposite bank, where clumps of bamboo grew, forming a shady arch over the path to the river.

He shrugged his shoulders. "That's superstition, Luz. If you hadn't seen it, you would never have known. Then what difference would it have made? Are you sure it's the bamboo?"

"Let's go and see!"

"Forget about it, Luz Marina," he replied, throwing a covering of canvas across the boat. "It's probably another bush in flower. It's not important anyhow."

Not wanting to spoil Salvador's mood, I averted my eyes from the bushes. But I thought I had seen it, and I remembered my mother saying that the bamboo flowered once in fifty years, and that it was a signal of bitter times to come.

Donã Catalina Riviero Casal, Salvador's mother, lives much of her life on the broad *galeria* of her house, on Avenue Cahal Pech. The house overlooks San Joaquín Church, where I was to be married, and the small plaza. Similar to others nearby, her house is a three-storey concrete structure with sloping zinc roofs. When it rains, water rushes from the gutters to enormous storage vats to the rear of her house.

On the mornings and nights before the festival to honour San Joaquín, our patron saint, the cool March air is filled with the smell of corn and meat roasting over charcoal fires. The cries of vendors rise above the plucking of guitar strings, and children splash each other with water from the fountain. Shoppers drift up and down the streets, examining costumes on makeshift stalls.

Marimba bands sometimes play. During the long heat of the afternoons, however, the small plaza is almost deserted.

Doña Catalina must be sitting on her *galeria* today, receiving the condolences of family and friends all over again, as upon the death of Salvador, and now because of my release. Perhaps she is thinking, "Thank God for my second son, Andrés, and for my grandchildren, who look so much like Salvador Joaquín."

At the trial I had seen that her straight hair was almost completely grey, trimmed short, curling around her ears. In all likelihood, she has today removed her marriage rings, and is dipping manicured fingers into a bowl of ashes before making the sign of the cross on her forehead. I feel sure that the crystal rosary beads moving through her fingers flash regular multi-coloured signals onto the whitewashed *galeria* walls. She may be blessing herself repeatedly, oblivious of the ashes smearing the skirt of her black linen suit that is lined with silk.

I think of going there to talk with her, to explain, but what is there to explain? What could I say? Would she look down at me through the alamanda vines intertwining the white ironwork grille which encloses the *galeria*? If she did, perhaps I could begin: "Doña Catalina, please give me your forgiveness. It was an accident of the time. I was not myself. I feel so sorry. How are my babies? Does the doctor still say Feliciano will never know us again? I cannot believe that. How is Teresa, our little flower? And Eduardo, our soldier, so brave, so big now, Doña Catalina, isn't that true?"

What would she say? Would she reply? Or would she gaze unblinkingly down at me with those large, golden eyes, so like a jaguar's when she is angry? Her face, usually round and rosy, is thin and haggard; her smile twisted and angry. I watch as she lifts her silver-headed cane, pointing to the distant hillsides, to far pastureland, to the tall cohune palms underneath which all of her dead lie in high tombs painted a glittering white. There is a slight hunch to her shoulders. She turns away, leading her guests across the pink and white tiles of the *galeria* to her sitting room.

White sheets cover the furniture today, I feel sure. The velvet on the chairs and sofas will be too red to bear. Double glass doors look out over the garden. She might sit there with family and friends watching hummingbirds dart in and out of the hibiscus bushes below. Rufina, barefooted, her long plait swinging, her thin white shawl sliding to her shoulders, would close and bolt the *galeria*'s giant ziricote doors.

Some time after I went to work for Doña Catalina, a *compadre* of hers began carving scenes on those doors, intricate images of their early life – when San Joaquín was still a village. On a day when Doña Catalina was in Belize City on business, he began carving a ruined Maya temple on one of the door panels. The following Monday, twirling his straw hat in gnarled hands, he told Doña Catalina about a dream. A spirit had instructed him to carve a Maya maiden being sacrificed on the temple altar.

"No maidens, and no more temples, please, Don Higinio," she said, pointing her cane at him. She called him Don to show she respected his work and was not angry.

The panels progressed slowly, inside and out, with scenes of women getting water from the well, villagers in their *milpas*, children swimming and mothers beating clothes on massive rocks in the Río Caracol.

One Saturday afternoon, when the doors were nearly finished, Doña Catalina and I went out on to the *galeria* after lunch. She sat in a cane chair, its rectangular back rearing almost a foot above her head. Don Higinio squatted inside the sitting room, working on a panel near the floorboards.

I wanted to confide in her about something, but I was afraid. I had heard her say to Rufina only the week before, "Please do not talk to me about Salvador Joaquín. He is my son and I love him, but every time he comes to this house we quarrel. He thinks I betrayed him and he blames me for everything." Once again Salvador must have disappointed her or made her angry about some important matter.

Off and on, for several years, I myself had tried to bring her news of Salvador's activities, if I had heard anything. Often she would simply incline her head to show that she had heard my words, but did not wish to continue the conversation. This day, though, I had something I needed to say.

My heart began beating faster as I sat in a chair beside her, my hands folded on several weekend newspapers. I began by telling her about Salvador's first visit to my parents on our *milpa*.

"And, Doña Catalina," I said, "Salvador brought the new pastor to meet Mamá Sofía and Papá Apolonio. He has joined the new evangelical church, and is trying to persuade my family to do the same!"

Doña Catalina looked surprised, then annoyed, but she did not reply. She left the *galeria* without commenting on the panel Don Higinio was carving. He was surprised and disappointed, so I stayed outside watching him work until the plaza lights threw the shadows of the church on to the *galeria* wall. During the years I worked in Doña Catalina's home, it seemed to me that she and Salvador had treated each other like bitter enemies. It is strange to think that it was his death which was the cause of their reconciliation.

Each time I remember the terrible look Doña Catalina gave me on the one day she attended the trial, I shudder with fright. From my fourteenth birthday to my twenty-second year, she had looked at me, most of the time, with such affection.

In spite of all she and I have been to each other in the past, the sad truth is that I know she would never answer if I dared to call from the street. And if I waited in the plaza, and if by chance we met there, and if by some grace of God she chose to speak, I can guess what she would say, as loudly as possible so that anyone who cared to could stop and listen.

"You always were brazen, barefaced and bold, Luz Marina. Heartless, without conscience, or you wouldn't even think of approaching me. So where is the famous smile that enchanted the judge and the jury? My family, and my church ladies, and even Rufina, agree that I succoured an Ixtabai. Regardless of what you now say Salvador did or didn't do, how come you didn't think of me?"

I would want to tell her, "I am no Ixtabai, Doña Catalina, and I did think of you, I think of you all the time. Please let me explain."

But I know such a conversation is a *fantasia*. It could never happen. It is very difficult for me to remember, and it feels more than strange to think I am not one of her family any more. I am not only outside Doña Catalina's home, but outside my old life, and everything I want so much. Besides, it would be too painful for her, too cruel of me. In court, the prosecutor told the jury that I had a jealous eye and a vengeful hand. Just imagine. Me. *Dios mío.*

I think of the probation officer, Mrs Wade, a nice lady, with silver hair and wide hips. The very last thing she said to me was, "If things go as I hope they will, please do not go there to harass the household. Be guided by your pastor. Give yourself time." Ah, time.

In bad moments I imagine I should give up, find a cotton tree in the bush and lay in wait behind it for ever, as they say Ixtabai waits to pounce on drunken but innocent men. This is how the people in San Joaquín will look at me, I know.

I can hardly breathe when I think about it, for I loved Salvador so, worked hard, and tried to please him. But, of course, I did not succeed.

When we first began to live together Salvador seemed to lose respect for me because I would not sell the little piece of land my parents bought, with their life savings, and gave to me when they thought Salvador and I would be married.

"You are three times crazy, Luz Marinita," Salvador said. "In my family we seldom place sentimental ideas over money."

In the end, because I was desperate for him to stay by my side, I allowed him to sell my land "for little or nothing", or so he said. I didn't understand then what he meant, but I do now that I have lost everything.

I can't believe myself that this thing has happened, and that Doña Catalina is my enemy for as long as we both live. I sometimes wish I could talk with someone about everything, but this is also not a possibility. It would take a long time for me to tell everything, even if I could, and it would take such patience to listen, and even the lawyer and the doctor are not interested in everything. Of course, to me, everything has a bearing on my case. It is my life.

So I must talk to myself, but I must remember never to move my lips because in San Joaquín we say that only people who are crazy talk out loud to themselves. And I am not crazy. I know that, although it is no thanks to Salvador, the father of my children. May his soul rest in peace, and if it doesn't, it is no thanks to me. I have promised a rosary for him every day as long as I live. It is a small thing but it eases me to do it. Perhaps I should do more, but I am not sure what. Perhaps I'll know some day.

Whatever they are, and Doña Catalina and her family are far from being saints, I am now considered to be worse, just imagine that. In choosing to live, I have lost my life, it seems. I pray it is not so. The lawyer taught me to use "it seems", and I like to use it now. It gives me a great freedom to think about things that seem to be, or seemed to be. Those are very good words. They help me so much. I have begun to collect small things that comfort me. I have about five already, not many, but they will grow in number I feel sure.

In the plaza, old men and women sit on iron benches under casurina trees shaped like umbrellas. If I sat there, somebody in Doña Catalina's household would see me and call the police. Different warders used to tell me that they are building a new prison far from Belize City, with a room waiting especially for me. The lawyer said they were only joking, but I pray never to see it.

In the small group of things that comfort me, I have my singing. As a girl, I sang in the school choir. In prison, when the noise of the other prisoners became too much, I sang the hymns that ask for God's forgiveness, hymns like "Amazing Grace". Sometimes the prisoners would sing with me; but other times, late at night, they called out, "Shut up, *loca*." And most of them were Creole and didn't even know how to speak Spanish.

But I forgave them all the names they called me, and everything they did to me, because it is as nothing compared with what I have done. My list of things to pray for, and against, gets longer each day.

There is always Doña Catalina who I must be careful never to offend in the slightest way for she has my children. In this extremity, who knows what Doña Catalina, and Rufina who feeds them, will lead my innocents to believe about me? It will be hard. But somehow I must find a way to at least see my children now and then.

In my heart, I feel like a good mother still, even though the court has ruled that I cannot have my children for some time. In my bravest moments, very few, I decide that I should not want my children. I decide that as the court does not seem to consider me a fit mother I should give them up; for their sakes since I love them so much, as Mrs Wade often reminded me. But at nights, before sleep, when reasoning seems pointless, I know that I want my children with me. I am bound and determined to become a fit mother again although I don't know how I will do that. But I will devote my life to it.

At least when the children grow up, they must hear better news of me, if they are not with me, but I pray each day that they will be. How I long to be with them again, to see them, hug each one, to sit near them, to cook for them again. Feliciano, Teresa, Eduardo. Their names feel like cool water on my tongue and in my throat. I was sitting with Teresa and Eduardo near the candles that always burn in the chapel of Our Lady of Sorrows, in the Church of San Joaquín, when the police found me that night.

Mr Reuben Oliver, the lawyer, opened the door of his car for me. From the back veranda of the courthouse, overlooking the sea, people were staring down at me. The lawyer looked at me, a question in his eyes. I had to go against his advice; I could not change my mind. I would not stay here in Belize City as he had advised me to do. I needed to be in San Joaquín, near to my children.

Every day there I would be able to soak myself in the Río Caracol. The stench of prison was on my tongue, on my clothing, in my hair, in my nostrils. Perhaps, in time, if I soaked for as much as an hour each day on the rocks near the waterfall, this stench would go away, but what could I do about the smell of death in memory?

Mr Oliver told me once that he'd prefer it if I called him a barrister. Sometimes I forgot, but he had become a sort of friend, now. This was a new experience for me, to know someone outside San Joaquín as well as I seemed to know Mr Oliver. He was a very courteous person.

"The bus station, please, Mr Oliver. I am sorry to give you more trouble."

"Returning to San Joaquín is an ill-conceived idea, Luz Marina." He used those words in court once or twice during my trial, but it was difficult for me to concentrate on the words of the lawyers. It was even more so with some of the witnesses from San Joaquín. "Wouldn't it be wiser, safer, to complete your probation here in Belize City?"

"I am sure you are right, Mr Oliver," I said.

I watched this new friend, short and round, putting his black robe and my small bag on the back seat of his car. He hesitated before getting in, jingling the keys in his hand. I knew he was worried.

"Mr Oliver, I am sorry to disappoint you, to go against your advice. But I need to be near my children."

He was reversing the car and did not reply.

"You understand?" I asked as soon as I could see we were on our way to Mosul Street where the bus station was located.

"I understand, yes. In any case, if you ever want to return, or need my help in any way, please let me know."

"I owe you such a lot already."

"Please do not feel you owe me anything," Mr Oliver said. "I am compensated through the courts, as I've mentioned before."

"I'll be very careful to do my service, and to report regularly," I said, smiling. "Please also thank your wife for helping me."

I thought of their young son arriving at the prison at noon every Sunday, with white enamel carriers filled with rice and beans, potato salad, stewed chicken, and a small baby-food jar of chopped onions, carrots and peppers in white vinegar. I was never very hungry there, and so most of my Sunday dinners went to other prisoners.

The Olivers are good people, and I thank God that the court appointed Mr Oliver to defend me. But I also have to ask God to forgive the small pain of envy I feel for the warmth of their family life. I envy every couple I see in the streets, every family strolling through a park. I do not remember being envious of many people before. Now enviousness has become one of my biggest faults.

Mr Oliver smiled in return, happy perhaps to see me smile. But inside myself I was not smiling. I had not smiled inside myself, the way I did as a girl, since the morning of the day when I was to be married.

On that Saturday, news came early that Salvador's younger brother, Luis Ricardo, had died in a traffic accident on the Hummingbird Highway the evening before.

Of course Salvador spent that day, and the weeks that followed, grieving with his family and helping Luis's family adjust to their terrible loss. I understood that. Still, in the light of all that has happened since, I am thinking of the bamboo flowers that I thought I had seen the day before.

I should have gone back along the path later, to check, to make sure I had seen them. But in those days, and for some time afterwards, I seldom felt it very necessary to prove myself right, in what I then considered to be small matters, especially if it meant having an argument with Salvador.

I kept my wedding dress for years afterwards. That was the most beautiful dress I ever had, so I took good care of it. Each Saturday I lifted it from the mahogany chest my maternal grandmother gave me before she died, and hung it on a special padded hanger on a nail over the window. There, it could catch the breeze from the river and stay fresh. I examined the folds carefully for mildew. I kept two green plastic clothespins only for pinning the veil to the dress.

After my housework was over for the day, I sat on the edge of the bed, admiring the appliquéd skirt blown into the shape of a barrel by the wind. The veil of bobbinet flew out like the wings of the angels that guard the doorway of the Church of San Joaquín. I imagined I was wearing it on my lost wedding day. It was a small Saturday pleasure to think back to the day that was to have been my wedding and to dream of the day it would return.

Salvador did not like me to go out of the house very much. At first I agreed with that, for I had a lot to do at home. But I missed going for walks to admire the gardens in San Joaquín, or shopping in the plaza. However, if I was not in the house when he returned home at any time of the night or day, he was always angry. I am not exactly sure why this was so.

Once he padlocked the doors and barred the windows so I could not leave. I had to remain there until he returned late in the evening. We did not have enough food in the house and the children cried. After the first time he did that, my trust in Salvador was never the same. I was always on my guard after that day.

Salvador always told me that on Fridays and Saturdays he had to visit Belize City to collect donations for the Evangelical Church. By now, he had won the confidence of the pastor and the congregation. I must have been simple, I truly must have been. Even the doctor said she was surprised that I was content to stay around the house and the yard day after day except for Sunday evenings when I went with Salvador to the church under a big tent in a field.

At first I didn't like the doctor assigned to me by the court. Dr Marjorie Anne Douglas is petite and slender, with a dark brown complexion. She has a boyish haircut, and small golden hoops in her ears. Her office at the Belize City Hospital is neat and welcoming, and she travels to the hospital in San Joaquín once each month.

I thought she wouldn't be able to understand how my life was. After a while, though, I think she began to believe in me, and to help me feel better. She didn't mind if I argued with her, or cried, or overstayed my time. The one thing she does not like is when I am quiet.

"This is exactly why everything piles up on you," she once said to me. "You should have confided in someone before things got too much for you."

"Who?" I asked her. "Just tell me who." She couldn't answer that question, of course, and really I didn't have anyone. Most women I know go through worse things than I did. I have only to think of my mother. I did want to join a sewing circle or the Mothers' Union. But when the leaders of these groups came to visit me, I found excuses not to attend their meetings. I was always afraid Salvador would return home unexpectedly and find us gone.

The doctor writes down everything I tell her. When next I visit her office at the hospital in San Joaquín, I want to be able to report that I have found a job or made some other small progress in this new life. She doesn't like me to repeat the same things over and over, although certain things seem to stay on my mind.

She gets impatient when I want to share comforting memories like the various recipes I prepared to tempt Salvador to eat his meals in our house. Salvador had several homes, including his mother's, and those of his friends, where he could eat his meals and attend parties and a variety of other functions. Often he did not return home for days. And when he did, I never knew what his mood would be, or when it would change. He didn't either, it seemed.

I forgot to tell the doctor about my wedding dress. She'll want to know about that. I stopped asking Salvador when we would get married, although I still wished for it with all my heart. It was always on my mind but I never asked, especially after I noticed he enjoyed listening to me beg. Although he kept his face serious, he seemed to get some satisfaction out of telling me that we would marry one day, but not just yet.

On the Sundays when Salvador was at home, he never minded if I took a walk, visited my parents or went shopping in the plaza, so long as I took the children with me. He sat, for most of the day, eating, drinking and talking with his friends in our small concrete block house, its kitchen shaded by a large mango tree. Five wide steps led down to the yard and the river beyond tumbling over huge rocks, boulders and stones.

When the children and I left the house that day for a walk across the suspension bridge over the Río Caracol, my wedding dress was blowing like a curtain at the big window in our bedroom. The glass beads and white sequins on the shoulders and sleeves sparkled in the late afternoon sunlight. It was a sight to see.

On our return, Feliciano and Teresa were falling asleep on their feet, so I didn't stop to say anything to Salvador and his friends. He didn't like me to enter the dining room anyway when his friends were there, unless I was going to take in more food or drinks. Whenever I served them, his friends would joke with me, praising my cooking with extravagant phrases. Then I would leave.

After putting the children to bed, I went straight to our bedroom to pack away the dress in tissue paper, and to replace it in the chest. The dress was gone! I couldn't believe my eyes. My heart pounded as I stared at the empty window. When I looked up, Salvador was at the doorway, holding a tumbler of whisky, soda and ice.

"It blew away, Luz." I didn't need to ask what he was talking about.

"How?"

"A strong breeze must have blown it through the window. By the time we saw it, it was already in the river. We tried to pull it to the bank with a pole from the clothesline, but it was out of reach. The current is so swift."

He was drunk so I knew better than to start an argument with him. Arguments with Salvador usually led to fights, after which he would leave the house. In San Joaquín some people believe that if a man beats a woman he loves her. But I did not believe this. I always tried to defend myself and taught my children to do the same.

"After a while, Luz, the dress sank into the water near the falls."

I sat on the bed and covered my face with the tail of my skirt, grieving silently for the loss of my dress. I didn't believe his story and knew that in some way I had offended him; it was a punishment, but for what I had no idea.

After a while, his friends left. Salvador came outside to stand beside me on the kitchen steps where I sometimes sat at night when the children were in bed. I listened to the river rushing past. At certain seasons it rose as high as the kitchen, flooding the floor.

"Forget about it, Luz Marina. I'll get someone to make you another one." He pulled me to my feet so that my head rested against his chest. "Draw me a pattern and I'll have it made up in Mérida. Or would you prefer one from Miami?"

He was teasing, so I didn't reply. I smiled although the tears were pouring down my face. After that evening he never mentioned the dress that blew away, nor the one he would get to replace it, and I never reminded him of his promise.

I couldn't imagine a more beautiful dress than the one which my mother and I had made. I was surprised to discover that I didn't even want another one any more. But I wondered constantly what happened to my dress that supposedly blew, according to Salvador, like a handkerchief through the window, across our small garden, and the neighbour's, to finally drown in the falls of the Río Caracol.

That same night I had a dream that has recurred often through the years. In the dream I was at my wedding, wearing the dress that drowned in the river. Guitar music was playing and Salvador and I were floating through the air over the jungles, the rivers, and the jutting hills. He was holding me tightly for I was afraid. Suddenly he let go of my hand, and I was in the middle of a strange *rancho* watching him marry the widow of his brother Luis. My wedding dress had turned into the white *huipil* which I use as a nightgown.

People at the wedding were staring at me, and when I walked across the grass to stand next to Salvador, he turned away to embrace his sister-in-law, kissing her passionately. I heard him say, "I love you so very much, Maria Elena. I will never let you go."

The air was thick with blue butterflies. Their wings fluttered against my face. I touched Salvador on the shoulder, lifting up our baby who was laughing and reaching out to him. But he wrenched my hair and threw me on to the ground and our baby disappeared and I found myself in one of the Maya ruins that are on every hilltop.

Inside the ruins were many narrow rooms with no windows. The people painted on the walls came to life. They pointed to a tiny slit in a wall. I looked through and everyone was on the *rancho* again. The guitars were still playing and Salvador was dancing with his sister-in-law. I felt a tug at my heart. Somewhere, someone was singing.

I squeezed myself through the slit in the wall and fell a long way to the ground. I picked up a jagged rock and threw it at

Salvador but I missed and he laughed. It began to rain. Thunder rumbled like a rockslide, lightning flashed and I was shouting, "More, more," to the wind and the rain, to the thunder and the lightning. I was blown higher and higher until I saw the sun, blue sky and white clouds again.

The music had stopped, the *rancho* was deserted, Salvador's house was in ruins, and I cried, "No more, no more, please," but the rain and wind began again and I found myself in our bedroom. I crawled into bed beside Salvador, and we were making love and I knew that he had forgiven me. He would never be unkind to me again; nor I to him. We were together for ever and I said to him. "I am sorry I destroyed everything but I was so sad that you didn't love me."

"I do love you, Luz Marina, my little *muñeca*. I've fixed everything. Forget about it."

It was true. Everything was as it had been. I had been so foolish. In my dream I went to a thatched room in the garden and began sewing costumes for the festival again; each costume a different colour, each one the same design as my wedding dress.

Whenever I woke from that dream, I resolved to try even harder to please Salvador. I believed the words of God in the Bible. I believed that even though I was only a common-law wife, I should obey my common-law husband, as I would obey God. I believed that the man is the head to which the woman's body is united, just as Jesus Christ is the head of the church.

I believed that a woman should be fruitful as the vine that climbs the walls of a home. I tried to live up to my beliefs, but, in most areas, I did not succeed.

Sometimes, although it seems like all the time, I wonder how it is that I have reached this low state in my life when I had meant it to be so different. I wonder if life will ever again seem all right to me. I may be wrong, but I sometimes think it has to do somehow with my Papá Apolonio. He had a terrible fight with José Alpuche Guerra one year at the festival.

For many people, the Festival of San Joaquín is a prayerful week of solemn processions, church services, candles and incense. For others, it is a time of unrestrained feasting, dancing, singing, drinking and fireworks. But sometimes the festival can turn, unexpectedly, into a time of despair, sorrow and danger.

On the final day of each festival, Mamá Sofía prepared for our family and for our guests, the Alpuche Guerras, an elaborate soup thick with onions, chicken and vegetables. We roasted whole plantains over coals, and made thick yellow corncakes. Perla and Concha squeezed large quantities of limes to make juice with water and sugar.

In those days, we lived about two miles from the plaza on the leased Casal land my father farmed. Our hut, made of pimento poles lashed together, was one of the larger homes in our area. The thatched roof kept it cool, and the walls were whitewashed. The bush surrounding the hut was cut back, and it was possible to stand beneath the cohune palms, or to chop hands of bananas from the suckers, without fear of snake bites.

As girls, my sisters and I often sat outdoors with Mamá Sofía admiring the heavy green fruit on the papaya trees. Each year we calculated how many should be left to ripen for sale at the market, or how many could be cut green, stewed in sugar and ginger, bottled and sold in the plaza. We kept chickens and pigs, and grew peppers, spinach, tomatoes and a variety of other vegetables.

Each year, including the one in which Papá had the fight, Mamá Sofía, Concha, Perla and I marched with the sodality in the religious procession on Sunday. We dressed in white, wore white lace mantillas on our heads, and carried lighted candles in paper cups. Praying our rosary beads, we wound up and down the narrow streets of San Joaquín.

This particular year, on the night before the religious festival, we went to a fiesta in the plaza where competing marimba bands played until late at night. My father always took part in the traditional dances, which everyone loved to watch. Every year my mother, who hated to dance, pleaded with him not to get too drunk, and if he did, not to dance. But he never listened to her advice.

"I have no sons, that's why he drinks and acts so crazy every single holiday," Mamá whispered to us as we dressed in the bedroom, the windows open to the cool night air. The sky was filled with stars.

That year, Papá was the drunkest man at the festival; everyone agrees about that. He insisted on drinking raw rum, the worst kind of liquor. If he hadn't started drinking before the sun came up, my father would never have done what he did, it seemed to me then. Now I am not so sure.

I don't drink hard spirits. So I wasn't drinking when, on another festival day, long afterwards, Salvador burst into my parents' home, and pulled me by my hair, naked out of the bathhouse. Our children were playing in the yard and saw everything. From my experience of that time, I know that my own brain can become drunk without liquor.

Nobody in my family knew exactly where my father got the idea, that particular year, of dancing in the festival with the hog's head in a huge loaf of bread under his arm. It made Papá seem like a stranger to us. My stomach turned over to see the dead eyes of the animal, the open mouth, and the blood soaking into the white bread.

Although he was dancing with a crowd of men at the plaza, Papá also seemed to be dancing in his own world, bending, swaying from side to side. His baggy white pantaloons and long white shirt became stained with blood from the hog's head. His feet were white with dust; his leather sandals caked with mud. He'd lost his straw hat and sweat plastered his shiny black hair against his skull and forehead.

We stood in the crowd on the edge of the plaza watching Papá as he danced up to the marimba band alone. Sometimes we could scarcely see him as he danced farther away with his friends. According to Papá Apolonio, José Alpuche Guerra, who was also drunk, kept saying things to him like, "Apolonio, aren't you a Christian?" or "In my family we don't dance with the hog's head any more," or "Throw that thing away, Apolonio."

"Maybe I'll forget I'm an Indian when I become rich like you," Papá Apolonio finally said to José Alpuche Guerra.

"It was only a joke," Papá Apolonio said to us afterwards. "I don't know when the words slipped out of my mouth."

But José Alpuche Guerra became very angry. He began wrestling with my father, trying to remove the hog's head from under his arm. But Papá Apolonio refused to let it go. Giving up, José Alpuche Guerra was about to move away when he said, "You and all your generations look exactly like that hog's head under your arm, Apolonio Bol Figueroa. You'll burn in hell."

Papá Apolonio said that he then became angry. He swung a rum bottle and broke it on José Alpuche's head; his blood spurted and a fight began. It was a free-for-all. José Alpuche, everyone agrees, grabbed a machete from a coconut stall and chopped my father so badly that he was in the hospital for weeks. I remember the shouting crowd and the policemen beating people back with their sticks.

"José Alpuche Guerra," Papá told us, as he lay in a hospital bed, "is one of God's fools. If he hadn't insulted my family, I would never have wasted a bottle of good rum on his ignorant head."

I don't know if Papá Apolonio ever told us the exact truth about his quarrel with José Alpuche Guerra. Sometimes Papá Apolonio said, "José Alpuche is a big man now, too good for his old friends."

But sometimes I wonder if the fight had anything to do with me. This thought adds to the guilt and grief of these later years. From prison, I wrote to Mamá Sofía telling her this thought and in her reply she said, "Here in San Joaquín we are always to blame, Luz Marina, whether we do or we don't. It must be our fate, a part of the good and the bad of our lives as daughters and mothers."

Up to that terrible night, José Alpuche Guerra and my father had been the best of friends for years. On certain weekends in the year they would go fishing together at the cayes in José Alpuche's boat.

Each morning, on one island or another, they would make special breakfasts of diced raw conch, hot peppers and onions. On their return, they would bring home bags of fish, conch and crayfish for our families, and for the neighbours. My father helped the Alpuche Guerras with the corn, beans and pumpkins on their *milpa*, and the Alpuches helped us.

While my father was still in the hospital, Mamá Sofía said, "Papá Apolonio continues to envy José Alpuche Guerra because of his five sons. Papá's heart is breaking because of the lack of young men in our family."

After my father returned home from the hospital, he could not work as hard as he did before. He also drifted away from his old friends. The bush began creeping nearer to our house, the pimento poles of our house leaned sideways, rain came through holes in the thatch, and food became far less abundant. Among ourselves, as we worked, we often joked about the time before

Papá's injury when we complained about things that really were only the very smallest disappointments of a home.

Everyone in my family knew I intended, after high school, to become a primary school teacher. I was hoping to attend the Teachers' College on Princess Margaret Drive in Belize City. But within a few months of the festival, I had to leave elementary school to help Mamá Sofía with the care of Papá Apolonio. I also did the cooking, chased after our chickens and animals, and learned to sew festival costumes to sell to the merchants in the plaza.

Eventually, Papá Apolonio gave up work altogether. He stayed in the house, getting more miserable all the time, begging drinks from his few remaining friends. Papá missed José Alpuche Guerra although he would never admit it. José Alpuche Guerra was like family to him, and to us. Papá and José Alpuche had grown up in another region to the north, far away from San Joaquín. They often exchanged stories and jokes about the relatives they had left behind.

"My father once inherited a little money, you know, before he died," Papá told us one afternoon. "But my father was old by then. He started buying common pieces of rock from passers-by, at a dollar a piece. In a year, every room in our wooden house was filled with stones. Eventually the house collapsed."

As he told his stories, Papá Apolonio rocked back and forth in a hammock outdoors. Today he was rolling, on to a piece of cardboard, a dozen yards of purple sequins for costumes, as a favour to Mamá Sofía.

On the same day Papá returned home from hospital, he said that he was not going to give José Alpuche Guerra the satisfaction of seeing him walk on crutches into the church of San Joaquín. Mamá Sofía, Perla, Concha and I continued to attend mass, but every time we returned Papá would say, "I could die here alone, for all you care."

We became so busy trying, without much success, to restore our old prosperity, and to take care of Papá Apolonio, that we stopped attending mass regularly, although we never stopped praying.

After Papá, I, perhaps more than the others, regretted his fight with José Alpuche Guerra. Less than thirteen at the time, I believed myself to be in love with Elodio, the oldest of José Alpuche Guerra's five sons. One year, at a Christmas Eve party at his home in San Joaquín, Elodio had given me a golden chain with a cross. I wore the chain beneath the blouse of my navy-blue school uniform.

One Friday evening, during a fierce game of fistball in the San Joaquín schoolyard, the chain broke and fell from my neck. Afterwards, my sisters and I spent a futile hour scratching in the dust with our fingers and with sticks until sunset. I didn't know what I would say to Elodio when I saw him again. But, after Papá Apolonio's fight with José Alpuche Guerra, I never had an opportunity to speak with Elodio again, although I sometimes glimpsed him in the plaza.

José Alpuche Guerra, Elodio's father, died a few years later. Perhaps to this day his family continues to say that Papá Apolonio hastened his death. I don't know if this is true, but I do know that when Papá hit José Alpuche Guerra with the pint bottle of raw rum, the life we had known before that incident also came to an end. I have heard that Elodio owns one of the largest ranches in San Joaquín. He is married, with many children.

During the time I was in prison, it became difficult for me to distinguish memory from dreams, from fantasy. Did Doña Catalina really have twelve green parrots, the colour of the emeralds she wore in her ears, at her throat and on her fingers? And whenever I admired their fine colour, did she say,

"Columbiano, Luz Marina, the very best, a wedding gift from Don Pablo."?

Don Pablo was not from San Joaquín. He was from one of the republics, Mexico, Nicaragua or El Salvador, and before that Spain, I think. He was lighter-skinned than we were, his hair was brown. Balding, he allowed his thinning hair to grow very long. He used hairgrips to pin the wisps of hair into a tiny roll at the back of his head whenever he had guests or was leaving the house.

He was short, had a small paunch, small feet and thick lips. On his pudgy fingers, he wore a number of rings. These he admired when he was talking with someone and did not want to meet that person's eyes. His moustache was bristly, drooping down on both sides of his mouth. He had a laugh that could be heard all through the house. All the servants feared his laugh, I think.

Did those parrots really squawk my name in Don Pablo's mocking tones? His Spanish was peculiar and I found it difficult to understand him. Sometimes, he spoke to me in English which I understood better, but it was not the Creole English that I knew. Instead of listening to his words, I often found myself watching him fling his hands about. I stared at his fat broad nose and his narrow eyes.

I sometimes doubt my memory when I recall the enormous gilded cages in which the parrots lived, swinging on their perches. The cages sat in a recess in the enormous foyer, near the curving marble staircase that led to a wide corridor, off which there were many rooms.

I don't know if these memories are true, because sometimes in my dreams the parrots turn into scarlet macaws with long red tails. They look at me scornfully with Don Pablo's eyes.

It used to be my task at sunset, so bright through the windows, across the fields and in the valley below, to cover the cages with specially bought hand-embroidered cloths that kept the parrots quiet until sunrise when I removed them again.

Did those big, muscular dogs imported from abroad really chase Doña Catalina across the pastures one morning? I must have been nearly fourteen then, and I remember the terror in her voice as she screamed for help.

I had been walking the two miles from our *milpa* to the plaza in San Joaquín, a journey I made many times after I left primary school. I went only on Saturdays, when the plaza was thronged with villagers, doing their weekly shopping, lingering near the fountain or sitting on the benches under the trees shaped into umbrellas.

I had learnt to walk without looking to the right or left, keeping my eyes on the dusty road. My right hand held the white enamel basin of *tamales* on my head. The steamed, tender rectangles of corn were filled with stewed pork or chicken.

My hair was parted in the middle, and rolled up in a bun on the top of my head. I wore my best long skirt, shiny red, and a white blouse with colourful embroidery around the neckline. I loved to feel the dust between my toes as I walked along the path between the high bushes.

Most of the way, I had the road to myself. Sometimes woodcutters, *milperos* on horseback or other villagers on their way to San Joaquín would pass on ahead of me. As I walked, I looked forward to reaching the end of the bush and the trees, to the place where the road widened. From there, I could see the mountains of our region, called El Pilar. The highest peak in our country is El Castillo, so far away that it seems blue-black on certain days.

It seemed like I had always known that most of the land through which I walked, for miles on both sides of the road, was owned by the Casal family who lived in a beautiful house, trimmed with gold paint, on Avenue Cahal Pech. Their house was only one of many beautiful houses near where I sat on a bench beneath the shade trees selling whatever we grew at home, or made on the fire hearth in the kitchen outdoors.

On all those trips to San Joaquín, except the day I saw the dogs chase Doña Catalina, I saw mostly what seemed usual. On this particular day, I remember seeing those terrible dogs, six or seven, hurtling their bodies across the fields, chasing Doña Catalina. She was running, stumbling, just ahead of them, towards a tree, across the yards and yards of ground.

The dogs were trying to bite at her ankles, springing upwards as if towards her neck; blood ran down her arms and legs. I too began to scream at the top of my lungs, "The tree, Señora, climb the tree," but I do not know whether or not she heard.

She was a small, slender lady with long, straight, shiny black hair. I was relieved when she managed to scramble into the branches of one of the many trees that grew all around. The dogs had pulled off most of her clothing, and she continued to move higher into the tree, screaming for help, her eyes fixed on the dogs trying to scramble after her. I was afraid she would fall. I looked around but there was no one to be seen.

I did the only thing I could think to do. I took the white cloths from my basin and waved them at the Señora still screaming in fear and pain, while the dogs ran barking around the tree. I did not know if she saw me. I hid my basin in the bushes and ran as fast as I could to the estate office down on the opposite side of the road. It took forever to get there, and I had a stitch in my side, and it took so long to explain. Eventually Don Pablo dashed from the office with a gun in his hand.

I ran outdoors and back along the path, to stand by the barbed wire fence, peering through. Don Pablo, with his workers in a pick-up truck, drove across the fields to the tree where the Señora clung to the branches, screaming at the dogs.

Don Pablo Cruz Casal jumped out of the truck, and shot them. It was a relief to see the terrifying animals lying still and silent on the grass, to watch the men lift the Señora down, and take her away. I heard the birds again, and the splashing water of the river.

I found my basin where I had hidden it in the bushes. I examined the food anxiously to see whether any animal had tried to eat it but, apart from a line of big black ants marching up the sides of the basin, all was well. I brushed the ants away, covered the basin and hurried to San Joaquín plaza. I did not want to miss my regular customers at the bus depot on Jade Head Avenue, not far from the market place. People visiting the town hall, the police station or the post office, close by, also bought from me.

That night I told my family what had happened that afternoon. They could hardly believe it. "Such a fantastic story," Mamá Sofía said. "The dogs are never let out during the day."

"It's a wonder you didn't lose your *tamales*. God was watching you," Papá Apolonio said.

"A wonder indeed, Papá," I said, placing coins and crumpled green dollar bills on the plastic tablecloth.

Concha and Perla were not yet home from school and I was glad. Picking my towel from a nail on the wall, I walked through the door to the bathhouse a few yards away, filling my bucket with rainwater from the nearby drums. I set the bucket down in a corner of the bathhouse where Papá usually stuck his machete in a crevice between the zinc walls and the cement floor. Pouring tin-cans of water over my hair and body, I soaped myself thoroughly, trying to wash away the memory of the afternoon. I knew that dogs could be dangerous, but never in my life had I heard of, or seen, a pack of dogs intent on killing someone. Life was large, indeed, as Papá Apolonio often said.

It was pouring with rain the day Doña Catalina sent a letter, and one hundred dollars, with Ducho, her driver, a man as short as a dwarf with long, flowing black hair and squinty eyes. Doña Catalina thanked me in beautiful Spanish, and asked whether there was any way in which she could help me, to show her undying gratitude for saving her life. She had also sent oranges, grapefruit, a slab of beef, and a crate of special laying hens. Perhaps we would now be able to sell eggs, very profitable in certain seasons.

Papá Apolonio said later that I should visit Doña Catalina one day to thank her for the gifts and to enquire about her health. Without speaking about it, I believed we would never ask Doña Catalina for anything in return. To me, the sorrow and shame of Papá Apolonio's fight with José Alpuche Guerra was still too close. I was only too glad that I had been able to help someone else.

"God should take this into account, Luz Marina, when my day of judgement comes." Papá was laughing, but I knew he was serious.

"Perhaps, though, Luz Marina," he said at teatime, "when you reply to Doña Catalina's letter, you might ask her to recommend you for a job. It's a big estate." He stirred his tortilla around in the bowl of black beans in front of him.

I was surprised and glanced at my mother. Mamá Sofía and I have the same mass of crinkly hair, streaked with brown, like polished black coral. The cast in her left eye was very pronounced. She looked at me thoughtfully for a moment and then said, "That might be a good idea, Luz. You are older now, and shouldn't be selling on your own in the plaza."

That night I lay in my hammock, listening to the low voices of my parents, glad that the horrible afternoon of the dogs had brought some respite to my parents from the constant worry about money.

I was fourteen years old when Doña Catalina invited me to her house for an interview. Rufina, sullen and moon-faced, with her plait across her shoulders, instructed me to remove my green plastic slippers at the door of the kitchen. The bright room seemed larger than our whole house on the *milpa*.

I followed Rufina through the dining room, up the marble stairs, on to a corridor as wide as a narrow lane, through a sitting room, to the *galeria*, which had beautiful paintings of foreign places on the whitewashed walls. Palm bushes and blooming plants in clay pots crowded the corners.

A rectangular table overlooking the garden stood at one end of the *galeria*. A number of chairs were scattered here and there. The Doña had only just completed her breakfast.

I noticed the slices of pineapple, bananas and papaya, the silver coffee pot, and the knives, spoons and forks with initials on them. She offered me some fruit. I was thirsty and hungry from my long walk, and would have enjoyed eating and drinking from the beautiful tableware, but I shook my head.

"Thank you, no, Señora."

She was silent for a while, looking at me from my head to my toes, which were covered with dust. I put my feet under the chair.

"I spend a lot of time out here now," she said. "I enjoy it."

"It's a very pretty place, Señora," I said, keeping my eyes down, listening to the cooing doves on the roof, smelling the sweetness of the air from the hills. The soft breeze dried the sweat on my forehead. My blouse, once starched and ironed, no longer clung to my back.

"Are you able to read and write?" Her eyes were on me, but I did not lift my eyes to hers. I felt shy, suddenly desperate for her to take me into her home. The fragrance from the freshly baked cinnamon buns with raisins was making me dizzy. I looked at the centre of the table where bougainvillea petals floated in a sparkling glass bowl.

"Oh yes, Señora. I reached Standard Six."

"Who was your last teacher, Luz Marina?"

"Sister Mary Jocasta, Señora. She will tell you I was first in reading and arithmetic. You can ask her." My heart was beating.

"I will see her at mass on Sunday, and I will talk with her about you."

"Yes, Señora," I said, hearing the clicking of her rosary as she removed it from her bag, tossing the beads from one long, slender hand to another.

"You have long eyelashes," she said. "I cannot see your eyes."

"Yes, Señora," I said, gazing into hers, large, a yellowish brown, which looked strange against her black hair. She was smiling.

"Your eyes are clear and honest, Luz Marina, but you are so thin, and so young."

"I am very strong, Señora," I said. "I have no illness. We are all thin in my family."

"How are your parents?"

"Papá is the same," I said. "He is not as he was, since the festival last year. He got into a fight with Señor Alpuche Guerra."

She looked down at her beads for a moment. "I heard about it."

"Mamá Sofía sends you her regards. She is well."

The Doña leaned back in her chair made of cane and shining wood. I sat on a straight-back mahogany chair opposite her.

"I really need someone who can be with me for most of the day. I too am not as I was since the day you saved my life. Are you a patient person?"

"I remember that day, Señora. I could try to be patient."

"If you came to live with us, you would sometimes need to be my eyes and ears."

I looked at the books and papers on a smaller table beside her chair. "I can't read very hard books, Señora."

"Are you willing to learn?"

"Oh, yes, Señora." I thought of telling her then that I wanted to be a teacher, but I didn't and the moment passed. I had saved exactly one hundred and fifty pennies in a glass jar, buried in the earth near the shed, to the rear of our house, where we cooked on a fire hearth under a zinc roof.

"I am sure that Sister Mary Jocasta will convince me to have you here, Luz Marina. But how will your mother manage without your help?"

"My sisters will help Mamá Sofía so she will be able to manage, I'm sure."

"Then I am certain we will see each other again. Already I like you. We have no daughters, only grown-up sons. Andrés, our middle son, and Luis, our youngest, own a hotel in the bush. Salvador helps Don Pablo and me to manage the estate."

"Yes, Señora."

"I am in your debt, Luz Marina, and I would like to help you and your family."

"Yes, Señora."

I had hoped Doña Catalina would think of asking me if I wanted to attend high school, but she didn't. I thought of Mamá Sofía getting up before the chickens and going to bed late. I thought of the days when I used to work with Papá Apolonio on the *milpa*. He and I used to pretend I was a boy, but we had to give up that game some time ago.

Our home was in disrepair. My parents were hoping that with my help, Concha and Perla would go to high school. They were smart and studied hard. "Another year or two," Mamá Sofía said to me before I left the house. "If we can just hang on until then ..."

After that first visit it was not long before Doña Catalina sent for me. The path from our *milpa* to San Joaquín town was quite muddy so it must still have been the rainy season. At first, it seemed to me, I had very little to do. I read to her, ran simple errands, and listened to stories about her life. Often we did less.

In the afternoons we sat quietly together on the *galeria*, watching people in the streets, our thoughts far away.

It is only now that I realise how much I learnt in those early weeks, and in later years, at Doña Catalina's house. Without the knowledge gained from her, I do not know what would have become of me while I was in prison. The sounds were unspeakable, night and day. The filth carried past my cell made me vomit into the slop pail, creating a permanent stench.

One of the warders described the gallows for me. I didn't know why he did that. Perhaps my smile annoyed him. That happens sometimes, even though I often smile so that people will feel better, so that they do not feel sorry for me, because that makes everything so much worse, and harder to bear.

The gallows was not far from where I sat in the corner of my cell. The mechanism that could take a life was unadorned, just ropes, and an open hole in the floor. I felt first amazement, then sorrow, then anger to realise that it was so ordinary, so final. But then I remembered my own actions so I smiled. I had been thinking like my old self, and I was no longer entitled to do that.

The guard must have misunderstood my smile, because he said, "A very clever piece of work it is. After they hang you, Miss Luz, the ropes are released and you fall into a coffin below."

I smiled at him, but he continued to look stern.

"You don't believe you will hang, eh? They hanged a woman here once. It was before my time, but they did it."

Sometimes there, when I woke up, I did not at first believe any of it had happened. I learnt in San Joaquín Primary School that Belize City is below sea level, and that much of that district is covered with mangrove swamp. The Supreme Court, Her Majesty's Prison, and even the Belize City Hospital, where I was born, are situated close together on different streets facing the Caribbean Sea.

I was born early one morning, and so Mamá Sofía named me Luz Marina, the light of the sea. Mamá Sofía told me that Papá was happy that she had given birth safely, but he said to her later that day, "She is a beautiful baby, but we always prefer a boy first, no?"

I had watched many bright dawns, from my cell, in that year. Each time, the glancing sunbeams fell on my bloodshot eyes with the sharpness of a machete swung with unimaginable strength.

Because of the seven years, perhaps a little more, I lived in Doña Catalina's household, I know something of the world. I did not want to die, nor spend the rest of my life in prison. Sometimes there, I said to myself, "I love the world. I do not want to leave it." This is how I felt sometimes, angry, full of energy, as though I had a choice. But on the days when we went to court, I often lost my courage and cowered in the remotest regions of my mind.

In front of the Belize City courthouse are stores, shops, banks and a small, ugly park. I know it is ugly because I compare it with my memories of Doña Catalina's garden which, for one thing, is several times larger. But perhaps I only think the courthouse park is ugly because idle people regularly gathered there to stare at me, and others like me.

Whenever I emerged from the rear of the prison van, I lifted my head, tossed back my hair and smiled. I walked between my guards up the steps and into the courtroom. Inside, I still concentrated on smiling because I could not bear to hear the story they told about me there. Sometimes I could not remember if it was true or not. "No," I sometimes said to myself. "I could never have done that."

Doña Catalina taught me to create a garden, to plan it all out, to arrange the plants and trees so that they appeared to spring from the earth naturally, gracefully. On fine mornings, when the other servants and I opened the green shutters of the white house, fresh air and sunlight filled the rooms. As I looked out, Doña Catalina's garden seemed to me to spread out like Eden, a paradise of birdsong, fruit, flowers, trees, bushes and shrubs.

At first I believed that Doña Catalina had always been a grand lady. I thought she had always lived the way she lived, the way I found her in her house on the Avenue Cabal Pech. But she laughed, her lips curving upwards like Salvador's used to do.

"Ah, Luz Marina, I appear so fine to you because you are an ignoramus from the back of the bush."

I wasn't offended. It was true. But I can hardly be so ignorant now. I believe that Doña Catalina would be forced to admit that during these past few years, especially the last, my knowledge of the world, in certain sad and terrible ways, has equalled her own.

"In my youth," Doña Catalina said to me one day as we worked in the garden, "I wanted to become a scholar of some kind, but in those days I didn't know how to go about it. So I became a businesswoman instead."

It was a surprise to everyone when Doña Catalina married Don Pablo, many years older than herself. In later years, when Don Pablo was hardly ever at home, she was still reading and learning.

It was rumoured in San Joaquín that Don Pablo had one or two other households in different parts of the country, but at first I did not believe these things, although I never liked Don Pablo, nor did he like me. Perhaps it was because Doña Catalina always kept me close to her side whenever he was at home.

Back then, in spite of her modesty, I believed Doña Catalina was a true scholar, in my eyes at any rate. Don Pablo didn't think she was, and, when he was at home, laughed at the books she read. He would often flip through her notebooks muttering, "Too, too incredible."

If I had enough courage, I would write down all my thoughts in letters to Doña Catalina. I believe she would read them with interest. She is like that, at least she used to be. Still, people change. I have only to think of myself to know. But perhaps she would place my letters to the rear of the iron safe, hidden in her wardrobe. She does that with her important documents, money, jewellery and other things she hates to see every minute of the day; like her wedding photographs, framed in silver. I had hoped, and worked diligently, to be a grand lady like Doña Catalina.

Mamá Sofía wrote to tell me, while I was in prison, that Papá Apolonio and herself are now living in a different house on the *milpa*, in an area called Esperanza. Our old home has been torn down.

The bus is nearing San Joaquín now. The air has become much cooler. In the distance the hills are blue like the carved lapis lazuli brooch Doña Catalina sometimes wore. I am beginning to feel anxious and frightened again. I tighten my scarf underneath my chin, remove my dark glasses from my bag, and put them on. I swallow one of the precious tablets the doctor has given me. There are thirty of them, one for each day. When they are finished it will be time to visit her again.

Part 2

It felt strange to be free, unmanacled, walking the three miles towards Esperanza where Mamá Sofía and Papá Apolonio now lived. The road was narrow, dusty, with thick bush and huge flowering trees blocking out the view of the hills. At a break in the trees I stopped to look down the steep bank at the Río Caracol slipping like silk over the boulders and rocks. I had missed it all. But what seemed oddest to me was that I felt as though I was walking towards Doña Catalina's home on the Avenue Cabal Pech, where my children now lived, as I once did. I longed to be there.

I was remembering an afternoon on the *galeria* with Doña Catalina. It may have been in May during my second year in her home. The sunshine had been unusually bright and the humidity became almost unbearable. At about five o'clock the sky darkened and we retreated to Doña Catalina's room to escape from the hail, the rain and the wind.

"A freakish storm," Doña Catalina said, as we stared through the windows at the giant trees in the garden bending under the gale force winds. I began reading a religious tract to her as she lay fully clothed on the high bed, her eyes closed against the sorrows of her life which I was only beginning to understand.

Under the covers, within easy reach of her small hand, was a large photograph in a heavy silver frame of her first husband, who she said had died from tuberculosis, or perhaps it was malaria, when Salvador was a young boy. A wooden rosary with enormous oval-shaped beads, shiny and smooth, hung over one of the thick, rounded mahogany bedposts. Doña Catalina's head rested against huge soft bolsters covered in white embroidered pillow-cases. As she listened, she ran her hand through the rosary beads, which made them rattle.

That afternoon of the freak rainstorm, I was startled when Doña Catalina interrupted my reading to say in a whisper, "Luz Marina, I am thinking of leaving San Joaquín for good."

"Where will you go, Señora?" I was alarmed because I had grown to feel a sense of security living and working in her home. My duties were sometimes heavy, but I had only to look down at the Plaza San Joaquín, where poor people slept on benches or on the bare cement, to appreciate my good fortune.

"Anywhere, so long as it is far away from San Joaquín. I don't want my money to wrap itself like a snake around my neck, and choke me to death, like so many of my enemies are praying it will do."

"Which enemies, Doña Catalina?" She didn't reply but I knew she sometimes included Don Pablo, Salvador and Andrés among her enemies, but not Luis, who I believed was the one son who, in his quiet way, returned her affection.

As we began the evening rosary, Doña Catalina sighed and said, "We'll leave next year, Luz Marina, you and I. We'll travel like royalty all around the world. We'll sail on the finest liners – aeroplanes are much too fast. We'll go everywhere, you and I, to Rio, Spain, England, France, Africa, America."

"You and I in a little house in Miami, Doña Catalina, with no long stairs. Perhaps with a *televisión*, Doña?"

"Perhaps with a *televisión* for you, Luz Marina; I don't care for it. But you are right, no more large houses. This one is a killer of women. What about an apartment with exactly the number of rooms we need?"

"Oh yes, Señora," I whispered back, for I had learned quickly that Doña Catalina was always afraid that the servants listened at her bedroom door. Quite regularly, especially at night, she'd send me to the kitchen for lemonade or hot cocoa. In this way I could report back to her what was happening in that big house.

As the months went by, Doña Catalina often talked of leaving for Miami or Rio or Spain. Sometimes, if it had been a particularly bad day, she would hiss across the room as I turned back the covers on her bed. "Next year we'll leave, Luz Marina, prepare yourself."

"Yes, Señora," I always said. By now, I was caught up in Doña Catalina's dream of leaving the house and prayed that her dream might come true. After a while, however, I understood that Doña Catalina was unlikely to leave San Joaquín permanently and, even if she did, it was doubtful that I would accompany her. It seemed obvious to me that Doña Catalina would take Rufina to cook and clean. Ducho, Rufina's husband, would probably go, too, for he was adept at performing duties other people sometimes found distasteful.

Doña Catalina's dreams of unending travel abroad was one of the pleasanter parts of her life, and, unlike her business affairs, I was the only person who knew of these secret fantasies. This made us comfortable conspirators whenever I brought Doña Catalina's morning coffee, if the previous night had been particularly bad.

It became a game we played whenever Doña Catalina and Don Pablo quarrelled, which was more and more often. Salvador and Andrés always seemed to side with Don Pablo, and the quarrel always seemed to involve buying land from *milpa* farmers at what Don Pablo called "the going rate".

So, since the fantasy seemed important to Doña Catalina, I accepted it for what it was, a pleasant diversion from everyday life. I entered into the spirit of play, and refrained from questioning Doña Catalina too closely about dates, and costs, and transportation, and packing boxes.

She seldom referred to her attack by the dogs, but I believe she worried about it constantly. Distracting Doña Catalina from what she called "uncharitable thoughts" became one of my most important, and secret, duties.

"My life is a trial," she sometimes said. "I feel like a prisoner in my own home. We'll leave, Luz Marina. Don't become too comfortable here." At other times when I reported some minor household theft she'd say to me, "We are little more than policemen in this house, Luz Marina. Get used to it."

Doña Catalina loved gold and precious gems. Some evenings she played with a large collection of jewellery kept in a voluminous, soft, wine-coloured velvet bag with leather straps. She kept the bag in a mahogany box, darkened by age. Now and again there would be a new piece, a brooch, a ring, a necklace or dangling earrings handcrafted in Mexico or Guatemala.

On those evenings there was no talk of America or Rio or Spain. It was all about Don Pablo. She spoke of him in a normal tone of voice, audible to anyone outside the room, or across the hall. She told me of his love for her, his generosity. "I would do almost anything for Don Pablo, Luz Marina. He is my father, my husband, my brother."

When Don Pablo had first arrived in San Joaquín and announced that he was going to plant citrus, his friends thought he would bring a wife from Mexico, or Guatemala, or El Salvador. But he didn't. Instead he married Doña Catalina, a widow with one son, Salvador. Through Doña Catalina, Don Pablo was able to buy hundreds of acres of land from the government to plant orange and grapefruit trees, and to build a factory in order to export the juice. He and Doña Catalina quarrelled all the time about the workers from across the border who worked in the orchards and lived on Casal land.

One Sunday after a breakfast party, Doña Catalina and Don Pablo were talking together in the sitting room with the red velvet sofa and chairs. I was walking along the corridor with an armful of fresh towels when I heard Doña Catalina say, "It's illegal, Pablo. You are not paying them enough. They live like pigs."

"Who are you, Santa Catalina, to talk to me about illegalities?" Don Pablo's voice sounded lazy, replete. "You are happy enough with the proceeds."

"You should discuss these matters with me," Doña Catalina said, her voice echoing in the enormous room. "I am a full partner."

"So I should," Don Pablo laughed. "But you seem to have a personal bodyguard these days. We are rarely alone."

"You know why that is."

"No, I don't. Tell me," Don Pablo said. He must have heard my footsteps for his shadow fell on to the wide, tiled floor of the corridor. He saw me entering Doña Catalina's room, and called, "*Buenos días*, Luz Marina." His voice boomed through the house. From downstairs the parrots set up a racket, squawking, flapping their wings, calling, "Marina Luz, Luz Marina," in Don Pablo's sarcastic voice.

"*Buenos días*, Señor," I replied, without turning my head. As I placed the towels neatly in the bathroom cupboard, my heart was racing. When I re-emerged, the enormous doors were closed, and the parrots were silent. Relieved, I ran quietly down the stairs to the kitchen. It was my first of many experiences of being frightened, without enough cause it seemed to me, at the timbre of a person's laughter, of Don Pablo's heavy boots on the tiled floor, or of his mocking glance as I sat with Doña Catalina on the *galeria*.

One of the first things Don Pablo did after he married Doña Catalina, to the amazement of the town, was to import a statue which, at his instructions, the workmen placed in the middle of the outside patio. It was a human-sized likeness of a woman, holding a basket of fruit in her hand. He never tired of telling us that it was a representation of the goddess who protected his possessions. He sat on the benches around the statue whenever he was reading, or smoking and drinking in the evenings with his friends, landowners like himself, or with the priest from the Church of San Joaquín.

I spent many months trying to figure out why he had married Doña Catalina. She was certainly a very attractive woman, but Don Pablo didn't seem to care for her company very much. Salvador and Andrés reflected his attitude whenever Don Pablo was around. To me it was strange and puzzling. It was only after I began living with Salvador in his house by the river that I grew to understand that marriages are made for many reasons. I was young when I worked in the Casal household and I looked everywhere for signs of love.

Upon arrival at my parents' new home in Esperanza, just after sunset, I stood outside peering through the window, feeling like a stranger. The bus had stopped several times before we reached San Joaquín town. By the time I had walked for thirty or forty minutes it was too dark to swim in the river. I had wanted to arrive home with my hair and body fresh; to embrace my parents with the stench of prison washed away. Doña Catalina taught me how essential it is to the spirit to be as clean, sweet-smelling and tidy as possible, no matter what else is happening.

In prison, difficult as it was, I tried to live up to this training. It has become more and more important to me every day. Perhaps it is because I have lost almost everything else. I had my own room at Doña Catalina's. In it I learnt the bliss there can be in privacy. My prison cell taught me to live alone, even under supervision, with my thoughts and my memories.

Through the window, I could see my Mamá Sofía sitting near an altar. The candles before the wooden crucifix on the wall were lighted for evening prayer. Mamá Sofía's hair was white now, bundled roughly on her back, and tied with a strip of black cloth. I could not see my father, who must have been in his hammock. A hurricane lantern hung from the ceiling. On the floor near the back door, I saw my father's tool bag. I thought of his machete, which had been an exhibit at the trial.

During a lull in the evening breeze rustling the leaves of the bushes and trees, I heard Papá Apolonio groan, and I watched my mother pick up an aspirin bottle and fill a glass with water from a white enamel jug on the table. She moved with the glass to the darkened end of the room. Mamá Sofía was wearing a loose black dress, and slippers made of thick black plastic.

In the old days, whenever I returned home, I simply pushed the door which was never locked, but tonight I could not do that. I knocked, listening to the silence. I knocked again and heard Mamá Sofía shuffling across the room to the door. "Perla?" Her voice was low. Papá Apolonio must have dozed off again.

"No, Mamá, it's Luz Marina."

When she opened the door, the blood drained from her face. She was thinner than I remembered, and a lot shorter. She had not heard about my release.

"It's Luz Marina, Mamá, I am free now." I waited for her to stretch her arms out to embrace me. I longed for it.

"Free?" Mamá Sofía said, "*Dios, Dios,* free?"

"Yes, Mamá," I said. Her body was trembling and tears rolled down her face. "You don't need to be afraid any more," I said.

"No?" She stared as though she believed that I was La Sucia, a foul, filthy spirit of a woman. We believe she lives near the river, and can cause fevers and delusions. Our people tell stories about drunken men who follow La Sucia and wake up to find they are sleeping on graves in the cemetery.

"No, Mamá, no." I stretched out my arms and gathered her against my beating heart, burying my face on her neck. "Oh, Mamá," I cried. "Oh, Mamá."

She pulled me into the house and closed the door swiftly, mindful of the harmful winds that sometimes blow at night. She continued to look at me as though something she feared had come to pass.

"Nobody came to tell me. We sold the radio," she said, lifting the hair off my face and looking into my eyes. Mamá Sofía must have been reassured by what she saw there, for she hugged me closely then and whispered, "But we don't count for much any more. We do and say things now that will surprise you. I am sorry for it."

I wiped the tears from my cheeks and smiled into her face, growing more familiar with every moment. "I feel so glad to be free, Mamá Sofía, so very glad."

"Sit, Luz. Are you hungry? I was expecting Perla so everything is ready, thanks be to God." We sat down at the table, covered with the red and white oilskin tablecloth I remembered from our old home. I scratched at a hole in the worn cloth where it fell into my lap.

"I don't have much appetite, Mamá Sofía," I said as she placed beans and chunks of bread before me. She uncovered a small plate of rolled corncakes, stuffed with boiled eggs, tomatoes and onions.

"You look like a ghost, Luz Marina, a ghost. Eat something." She poured hot black tea into a white enamel cup with a blue rim, sweetening it with condensed milk from a tin. The room was gloomy and stuffy, smelling of bay rum, camphor and the herbs my mother boiled to massage my father's legs and arms. I was afraid to ask about Papá Apolonio's health.

"I thought it was Perla at the door," my mother said again. "She wrote me a letter to expect her at any time." She fell silent, and then began to weep, her bosom rising and falling. Every now and again, she said, "*Dios*, help me."

"Are you sorry I am here, Mamá Sofía? I can go back to Belize City in the morning." I looked down at my tea and saw a small dead cockroach floating on the surface. My stomach heaved.

Usually Mamá Sofía screwed bits of paper into the two openings of the condensed milk tin, but the cockroach must have crawled into the can before my mother had secured it. Now I saw that the table was filthy, and the floor littered with scraps of food.

"I am not sorry to see you, Luz, and I am glad you are out of gaol, but I think you should go back to Belize City. Everything is different since that night. Concha, as you know, doesn't feel able to return home, even for a visit."

Something rubbed against my leg and I jumped, spilling the tea across the table. My mother untied her apron and mopped up the liquid dripping on to the dirt floor.

"We have a cat now, to keep away the mice," Mamá Sofía said, letting the cat through the door. Then she said, "Papá Apolonio is not getting any better. A nurse comes sometimes to give him injections for the pain. She says he should be in hospital, but Papá doesn't want to go. He wants to die, so he says."

"I want to stay, Mamá," I said, walking to the hammock to look at my father, who was sleeping. He was emaciated, his hair and beard white. The hammock was slung low and, despite the lack of air in the room, he was covered to his neck with a thick blanket. "Have you heard any news about Feliciano, Teresa and Eduardo, Mamá Sofía?"

She shook her head. "But I don't worry about your children. They are in the care of a grandmother who can provide for them. Feliciano was taken to see a doctor in Mérida. Papá Apolonio and I did the best we could for them, after you left." She saw the tears rolling down my face, and said more gently, "But, of course you want to be close to them. That's only natural. You were always a good mamá."

Mamá Sofía came to my side, pulling my head on to her shoulder. "Apolonio, my Polo?" she said softly, placing the back of her other hand on his forehead. "The fever is not so high now. Polo? Apolonio?"

My father grunted, coughed, opened his eyes, and then his mouth, expecting food or medicine.

"Apolonio, listen to me." Papá Apolonio closed his mouth, and my mother drew me into the light of a second lamp on a wooden crate cluttered with herbs and medicine bottles. "Look, Apolonio, Luz Marina is home. She's free."

An incredulous look crossed Papá Apolonio's face and he removed a skeletal hand from below the blanket. "They aren't going to hang you, Luz?"

"No, Papá, I am not going to hang." I kissed his forehead.

He closed his eyes, then opened them again, "Who is going to hang then?" His mouth twitched and he placed a trembling hand up to it.

"Nobody, Papá."

He lay very still. I knew he wasn't asleep, but he didn't open his eyes again. I looked at his heaving chest, and at my mother's frightened face. My Mamá Sofía and my Papá Apolonio both seemed to be afraid of me; just think of that. It was hard to bear.

My memories shifted, interlocked; I fought against certain thoughts. My head bowed, I stood before my parents trying to recall my childhood. I seemed to remember leaping without fear from the branches of ancient trees growing thickly on each bank of the Río Caracol near our old *milpa*.

The trees grew so high and so wide that they almost obscured the blue of the sky. With our friends, my sisters and I, in those days, swam naked and unashamed. Our laughter sent dozens of birds flapping in noisy confusion through the branches. It was hard even for me to believe that memory, but it felt as though it is true.

In those minutes, I longed to be fifteen again, sitting in Doña Catalina's garden under one of the *guanacaste* trees on a Sunday afternoon, listening to the wind in the leaves, reading before it was time to help Rufina in the kitchen. Rufina spent her days creating special meals to please everyone, especially Don Pablo, for whom I think she would have given her life.

Don Pablo shouted Rufina's name the moment he entered the house, confident that she was there to reply. As he sank down in the hall chair, Rufina gently eased off his boots, replacing them with leather house slippers. Don Pablo was always gruff with Rufina, but I believe he cared for her as much as he could care for anyone in the house on Avenue Cabal Pech. Sometimes he would join the fingertips of his hands together and say to her, "Rufina. Your face tells me that you are missing our old house on the estate."

"Oh no, Don Pablo," Rufina would say, examining the muddy boots in her hands.

"Yes, Rufina, you can't fool me."

"If you say so, Don Pablo," Rufina would reply, her face bright with pleasure.

"I say so, Rufina," Don Pablo would say, retrieving his papers from the table in the hall. "I hope you cooked something good today, Rufina, and did not spend your time loafing about the kitchen?"

As he climbed the stairs, Rufina laughed at such an idea, covering her mouth with her veil. Every Sunday she made Don Pablo's favourite meal, a *relleno*, filled with tender pieces of chicken and pork, fragrant with spices, the white of chopped hard-boiled eggs speckling the thick black soup.

Rufina's inestimable value to the Casal family was without question; Doña Catalina and Don Pablo never disagreed about that.

Most of the time, I did not have very much to say to any of the other workers, except Rufina, who told me what to do, and then only when she was in the mood to talk, which was seldom. Doña

Catalina told me that ever since Rufina was quite young, she had what Doña Catalina called "sometime ways", and that I was not to take everything she said, or her silences, to my heart and worry.

At first, I did not think, however, that Rufina approved of the long hours Doña Catalina required me to spend with her on the *galeria*, since as the months went by I was needed to work as hard as Rufina did most days.

In the mornings I rose at five o'clock, sometimes as early as four. It took me some time to bathe and dress myself in the neat and modest way Doña Catalina required of someone who would sit with her on the *galeria* in the afternoons. Some mornings, especially on Sunday, I accompanied Doña Catalina to mass at the Church of San Joaquín.

Every day I helped Rufina to prepare breakfast. Then, if necessary, I helped to weed the kitchen garden, shopped and, on my return, peeled and chopped fruit and vegetables for lunch and dinner. About ten o'clock on certain mornings, I followed Doña Catalina and Rufina around the house as Doña Catalina inspected the rooms and cupboards. On other days I sat in the pick-up truck between Doña Catalina and Salvador, who drove us around the citrus estates on the outskirts of San Joaquín.

On those days Doña Catalina often spent hours in the estate office with Salvador, Don Pablo and other staff members going over the account books and other matters. I waited with the receptionist in case I was needed by Doña Catalina for personal errands to the house or elsewhere in San Joaquín town. Ducho often drove me to the drugstore or to the shops which sold imported foods.

To do Rufina full justice, I did not blame her for having "sometime ways" because of the variety of moods in the house. A house, it is said here in San Joaquín, has, depending on the circumstances surrounding its construction, the power of destroying the families who live in it. Of course, I for one do not believe that a house can cause a family to disintegrate. But I was beginning to wonder about the house that Doña Catalina and Don Pablo built on Avenue Cabal Pech.

I rarely knew where I was from one day to the next. On some days everybody was friendly, shouting and laughing. On those days I felt more cheerful, but at nights I was totally exhausted and could not do the reading which Doña Catalina insisted that I did every day and which I was eager to do. At other times the house was as quiet and empty as the nearby Maya pyramids of crumbling limestone rearing high above the bushes and trees. On the silent days I had more time to sit on the patio off the kitchen.

The dwarf coconut trees formed a canopy over the long wooden table where the servants ate during the good weather. I would try to read and write, conscious all the time of Rufina's scowls, expecting her to shout for me at any minute.

On one of those days, I couldn't concentrate on what I was reading so I went into the kitchen to help. But all the while we worked Rufina was mostly quiet, merely grunting her orders, instead of shouting at me for innumerable stupidities. She stood before the giant gas stove of stainless steel muttering to herself about matters which I did not understand.

It seemed to me that it was a worse silence than usual, the kind that makes you think something terrible has happened, or is about to happen. Doña Catalina had not come out of her room since breakfast time yesterday. She ate there, and then very little. Don Pablo was away and nobody knew for certain when he would return.

By then I knew that Don Pablo and Salvador often drove around the countryside looking for cheap land to buy. At other times when Don Pablo was away, nobody knew for certain where he had gone. He simply disappeared for weeks at a time, and then turned up again, as if nothing had happened. I worried when Doña Catalina was not about, for her absence placed a greater responsibility on me. In spite of what Doña Catalina expected, I did not have enough eyes and ears to watch everyone and everything. Even when I did hear what the servants were saying, I did not always understand.

One night, shortly afterwards, the servants were eating in the kitchen. It was pouring with rain, so it must have been in June or July. One of the outside guards, Pescador, said, "Maybe Sucia got Don Pablo in the jungle." He laughed, cleared his throat and fell silent.

He was called Pescador because he had a fishy smell about him. Ducho, the driver, didn't smell like fish, but I'd always thought he looked like one. His long, flat mouth was always opening and closing. Because Rufina seemed loyal to Ducho, I needed to be careful to always keep my thoughts about him to myself. Pescador was somehow related to Ducho.

I think they were more comfortable before Doña Catalina brought me to the house. They believed that I carried tales to Doña Catalina as I did. Still, I tried not to offend them unnecessarily. I was determined to hold on to my job because of my lame Papá Apolonio; for Mamá Sofía planting, cooking, washing every day; for my sisters who walked to San Joaquín School in sunshine and in rain.

That night, Rufina placed a second bowl of *escabeche* in front of Pescador, spilling a little of the hot soup on his lap. Of all of us, he ate the most but he remained long and lanky. At the table I sat very close to Rufina because Pescador rubbed his feet against my own whenever he got a chance. He picked a strand of onion off his khaki trousers and threw it through the back door to the dogs bought to replace those Don Pablo had shot.

They were kept in a large enclosure some distance from the kitchen and let out only at night to roam the estate. The new dogs immediately set up a commotion, barking and running around, expecting to be fed. None of the servants, in my hearing, ever referred to the old dogs who were so suddenly loose in the fields on the day when Doña Catalina was attacked.

"You and I will never be rich, Pesca," Ducho was saying. "Don Pablo now, he knows how to turn steaming jungle into cold cash."

"He calls it Belizean gold," Pescador laughed. He was always laughing; spit bubbled at the corners of his mouth. "Don Pablo's never been gone this long though, eh, Fina?"

Rufina frowned, then said to me, "Isn't it time to check on the Señora?"

Ducho glanced at Rufina's worried face and said, "We're fishing in troubled waters, Pesca. Let it go."

I left the kitchen, climbed a flight of stairs and walked along the wide corridor to Doña Catalina's room. I rapped quietly in case she was asleep but she wasn't. Pushing open the door, I saw her going through a pile of papers on her desk.

"Luz Marina? You and I are going to mass tomorrow in the evening. Ask Ducho to tell the padre that I will visit him afterwards."

"Yes, Señora. Are you ready to eat?"

"No, thank you. I won't need anything more tonight."

When I returned to the kitchen the others were finishing their meal. I gave Ducho the message. He nodded, but Pescador said, "The padre is very busy on Sundays, no?"

"He won't be too busy to see Doña Catalina," Rufina said. "He is a good man and Don Pablo's friend."

Pescador picked his teeth, looking speculatively at Rufina. "Well, I'd better get back," he said, putting a three-legged stool under the table cluttered with dishes, pots and pans.

The men continued their conversation briefly outside in the rain, before separating. I looked down at the grease congealing on the top of my soup. The dogs were still growling outside the door.

Rufina scraped the leftovers into the huge tins from which the dogs ate. Like Rufina, I was a servant in the Casal household, but I never considered myself only that, which was a mistake, of course.

That night, when I went to my room, next door to Rufina's, I noticed that Don Pablo's leather slippers were still waiting in the hallway.

On one of my many visits to the doctor while I was in prison, she told me that there is a certain emotional age beyond which many people seldom grow. I found this astonishing, but as I thought about it, I began to understand. In my heart I sometimes feel like fifteen, the age at which I began to love Salvador.

"Did Perla come home with Luz Marina?" Papá Apolonio asked, attempting to raise his head from the small cushion in his hammock.

"No, Apolonio. But she's coming very soon."

"That's good," my father said, grasping my mother's hand. "You shouldn't stay here, Luz Marina. Things are bad for us now, very bad."

"She will stay for a while, Apolonio. Are you thirsty?" He nodded, and my mother placed a straw in a glass of water and knelt by the hammock while he sipped. He smiled feebly at us, and closed his eyes. My mother turned the wick of the lantern down.

The following morning, my second day in our new home, I got out of my hammock before sunrise, but my mother was already up. Mamá Sofía was lighting the coals on the outside fire hearth to boil water for my father's medicines and for tea. Like me, she had not had much sleep.

Ever since I can remember, I hated to go to the outhouse in the dark, even though I always carried a hurricane lantern with me. I feared so many things; a snake would drop from the roof and squeeze me to death, a vicious animal would spring up from the pit latrine and pull me down into unspeakable depths. Evil spirits, who have lived in our region since time began, would cast a bad spell on me. Sometimes I believe they actually did, although it happened when I was completely unaware of their presence.

All these horrors came over me as I washed myself as best I could resolving to go to the river later in the day. In the Evangelica Church we believe that if you bathe in the river, and pray, you can be born again in Jesus Christ.

As I began to dress, my gestures were too urgent, too angry. This was a new day, I reminded myself, not that other day; Salvador could not rise from the dead, may God be merciful to him, and to me. I was fervently praying to be born again. I needed a new life. Really. I felt my skin burning with a sense of injustice mingled with pity for my parents.

I reminded them of what we wanted to forget, and I wondered what I could do, and where I could go. I returned to the house resolving to tell my parents how much I loved them and then depart. But I did not want to leave them in anger. They needed to forget me as much as possible; at this moment I needed to forget myself. I thought of my beautiful children. Feliciano, my first son, was twelve now. Teresa was ten years old and Eduardo was nearly six. It would be hard to leave them.

After we attended to Papá Apolonio, I sat at the table determined to tell Mamá Sofía that I had decided to go back to Belize City after all. She was waiting impatiently for the nurse who made her rounds early. I wanted to tell my mother all that I was feeling, but I could see that she was in almost unbearable mental pain. Her head was bent over a mug of weak tea. Her hand crumbled a day-old tortilla into tiny pieces.

"I don't know what I have done in my life to deserve this fate," she said. "Papá always said it is because we have no sons to protect us."

I laid my hands on hers and she grasped them. I searched my mind desperate to ease some of her pain. "Mamá Sofía, I had to see a doctor while I was in prison. In a few weeks I will see her again. She says that when there are no sons, it is not the woman's fault. I don't know if it is true."

"Your Papá Apolonio would laugh at that idea." She glanced towards the hammock, and sighed.

"You can laugh now, Mamá."

"Ah, Luz Marina, Luz Marina," she said. "Will we ever truly laugh again, you and I?" She glanced through the window. "Oh, my good God," she said. "Not so early!"

I saw with shock that Ducho, Doña Catalina's driver, was approaching the house. My mother did not seem surprised, only annoyed. "He comes here every week," she said. "They want us to move. Go out the back, Luz Marina. Close the door. I don't want Doña Catalina to know you are here."

I did as she asked, listening as she unbolted the door.

"*Buenos días*, Señora. May I enter?"

"My husband is no better, Ducho, worse if anything, so we are unable to move just yet."

"I am sorry to hear that, Señora, but I hope you understand that I am only doing my job."

My mother did not reply. I guessed that she was standing in the doorway, preventing Ducho from entering the house.

"This letter is for you, Señora," Ducho said. "From Doña Catalina's lawyer. Do you want me to read it to you?"

"No thank you," Mamá Sofía said. "And I don't need another letter to tell me again that we must move. We'll go when my husband is better, and we'll be glad to leave, believe me."

There was silence. I heard my mother bolting the door. Calling to me, she went to the window, watching as Ducho drove away. Her hands shook violently. I picked up the brown envelope from the table.

"Read it," Mamá Sofía said. "We are to leave in one month or face legal action. That's what it usually says."

"You are right, Mamá Sofía, that's what it says."

She pointed to a basket on the ground near the altar. "Throw it in there with the rest. I don't know what we will do. The money Perla sends isn't enough to rent another place, not with the amount we spend on food, and medicine for Papá."

"I'll get a job," I found myself saying, "and find us a place to live."

Tears were streaming down my mother's face, and there was a bitter smile on her lips. "But who would hire you here, Luz Marina? Have you forgotten what San Joaquín is like?"

"No, Mamá Sofía, I have not." I wiped the tears from her cheeks, concentrating on the San Joaquín that Salvador taught me to love, especially the nearby hills, covered with trees and plants of every description. I tried to remember the gurgling of the streams, the rushing of many rivers, and the waterfall in the mountains farther away, that drops into the river a thousand feet below.

I thought of the cold, sweet air of the Mountain Pine Ridge where I had hoped Salvador and I would one day live; of the hotel we would one day own there. But perhaps it had only been another one of Salvador's grand ideas; perhaps it would never have come to pass. Still, it seemed real at the time, and I believed in it. If I told the doctor about this dream, perhaps she would ask me gently, "You still believe in this dream, that it would have come true had you been a perfect wife and mother?" Perhaps she would look at her notes and say, "Didn't we discuss recently Salvador's unreliability in financial matters?"

"He was good to us sometimes, when he was well," I would perhaps reply, knowing I could never explain how mesmerised I had been by the beauty of Salvador's face, the sweetness of his smile, his laugh of satisfaction when he gazed at Feliciano, Teresa and Eduardo, who look so much like him.

I don't think I should mention to her the expensive pair of hand-tooled leather boots Salvador bought for me in Guatemala when we were first courting, and he thought he could love me. The doctor doesn't like me to dwell on the material things that were, for a brief while, so much a part of my life with Salvador.

Salvador was often so restless. He liked to walk for miles. So, during the first years we lived together, whenever he was at home, we would spend a lot of time outdoors. The children and I grew to love these excursions because Salvador was very knowledgeable about the jungle, the birds, animals and caves. He loved everything natural, and served for a while on a conservation committee at the urging of Luis's wife, until as was usual in our lives, Salvador became bored.

"The endless bureaucracy is too tiresome," he said, the night he decided to stop attending the meetings. I believe though that he had also become too embarrassed to return. To please Luis's wife, he had asked Don Pablo to donate certain acres to the government for a park. Don Pablo had laughed and said, "Too, too incredible. I cannot believe this is your idea, Salvador. You are never sentimental."

The parrots in the foyer heard Don Pablo's booming voice and repeated, "Too, too incredible."

"You are an old fool, Papá Pablo," Salvador had said, furious at being thwarted.

"Too, too incredible," Don Pablo said, laughing again and slapping his knees. "Maria Elena is a smart woman. I must ask her whether or not I am a fool, or whether you are, Salvador."

"You owe me this favour," Salvador said.

"I owe you nothing," Don Pablo said, "not now, not ever."

And so the relationship between Salvador and Don Pablo became strained, and Salvador was forced to look elsewhere for additional income to meet his many needs and obligations.

Still, the jungle continued to be a special place for the children and me, because there all Salvador's attention belonged to us. He knew the names of the rivers and the caves, and unbelievable stories about the ruins on Casal land, some of which looked to us like piles of rubble. As people say, those were the days, bountiful, brief, and long gone, except in my memory. I mourn their loss.

In a crowd, Salvador had a disconcerting way of addressing, if he was interested or fascinated, one person in any gathering to the exclusion of all others. If you loved Salvador, as I did, this exclusion from his attention even for a short while was extremely painful. I was often jealous, particularly of beautiful, educated women like the wives of his brothers, Andrés and Luis.

When we were with them, it bothered me that I felt like the maid; it seemed to me, at the time, that they also treated me like one. But if I tried to explain how I felt, Salvador always said, "That is a *fantasia*, Luz Marina. You have an inferiority complex, I think. Forget about it. Try to relax."

But I couldn't forget, and, with a self-confidence I lost somewhere in our relationship, I continued to complain about the fact that I felt ignored when we were with his family and friends. One Saturday evening, as we were dressing to go to Andrés's house for dinner, I tried to discuss my feelings with him in advance. He held my shoulders and said quietly, a dissatisfied tilt to his thin wide lips, "Don't accompany me tonight then, Luz Marina. I mean it." And he did mean it, not only for that night, but for nearly always. I couldn't believe it. Apart from the church, we rarely went anywhere together in public after that night.

Salvador entertained, on behalf of his family, government officials, diplomats, friends and business colleagues at the house on Avenue Cahal Pech. This was Salvador's special role in his family. His charm, and ability to persuade others to his way of thinking, brought the Casals great favours and benefits for which he never felt adequately compensated.

When he wanted to be, Salvador seemed to be automatically in command of most groups. All eyes went to him then, as though to the centre of life. His friends, like myself, sometimes went to great lengths not to incur his displeasure. His scowls and sulks, and it could be over the slightest thing, were frequently ferocious, and of long duration.

He had the ability to diminish a person, to reduce them to non-beings in his world, by a sidelong glance or a flick of his elegant hand. I believe Salvador knew that he had this power, and he had no hesitation in using it, if necessary, all day, every day of his life, God bless his soul.

In San Joaquín we believe that it is wrong to speak ill of the dead, so I do not feel able to tell the doctor all my thoughts. The Salvador I loved could be kind, gentle, generous, helpful. Whatever he wanted at the time, he pursued with a convincing passion.

But sometimes he was unsuccessful, as when Doña Catalina consistently refused to allow him control of her financial affairs. Then, his anger was unleashed with no restraint. If I said these things to the doctor, perhaps she would speak to me even more softly and ask, "But you believed that with you Salvador would be different, that in your care he would change?"

"Yes," I would say to her. "I had no experience, you understand?" I wonder if I could find the words to explain to the doctor how I felt when I discovered that Salvador despised ordinary people, even those he found useful, who served his needs.

I am rehearsing this conversation with the doctor in my mind, needing to tell her, but unable to decide whether or not there is any reality in what I am thinking. Through the doctor, I am beginning to understand that, often, I see what I want to see in the people I care about, like Doña Catalina and Salvador; my habit is hard to break.

Seeing Ducho again made me think of the November evening when Salvador's brother Luis Ricardo became engaged to his cousin Maria Elena Barrios. I was putting on my green skirt and white blouse when Rufina came to the door of my room. In her hands were strings of jasmine she had cut from the vines that grew against the kitchen door.

"For your hair, Luz Marina," she said shyly. In spite of her miserable ways, Rufina seemed to care about me. "Let me pin them into your plait," she said.

As she worked on my hair, she asked, "Why don't you put on the new white dress your mother sent to you? A virgin should always wear white on her fifteenth birthday, as every mother knows. Tonight you can pretend it's your party, your *quince años*."

"How did you know?" I asked, surprised.

"Doña Catalina mentioned it to me. She wants you to enjoy what is for everyone a happy occasion."

At the party Rufina and I were busy for hours serving food and drinks. Then we listened to the many fine speeches made by the families for the happiness of Luis and Maria Elena. Ducho, Pescador and the other helpers cleared away the dishes and the music started again.

Rufina and I went to sit on chairs near to Doña Catalina and Don Pablo. Lights were strung on almost every tree around the patio. Don Pablo's stone goddess wore a crown of little winking fairy lights. A full moon sailed through the clouds, and the breezes were soft, cool and sweet-scented.

Even so, the perfume of the tiny white flowers in my hair was strong in my nostrils. Salvador, Andrés and Luis danced almost constantly in the throng of happy people, young and old, on the patio of white tiles. The guitar music tugged at my heartstrings, and the drumbeats made me feel like dancing too.

After some time, Salvador came over to speak with his parents;

then he was bowing over my hand. "Everyone tells me that today is your birthday, Luz Marina. Why are you refusing to dance?"

Doña Catalina was smiling. "Yes, Luz Marina, at least one dance." Don Pablo pretended he did not hear.

"I have never danced at a party," I said to Salvador, as we walked from the grass on to the tiles.

"Then I am honoured," Salvador said. "I will show you. It is really quite easy."

I don't think I have ever enjoyed guitar music as much as I did that night, or danced with such grace or felt so beautiful. Perhaps everyone feels this way at fifteen. I don't know. I am short, and in those days I was as thin as I am now. As we danced, I didn't quite reach Salvador's shoulders, so he bent over me, his chin resting lightly on my head, one arm around my waist, my palm resting on his open hand. One of the guitar players began singing, and everyone sang with him. In my ear Salvador was singing, "the girl that I love is a little brown girl because she dances *la bamba*".

I was intoxicated with the night, the music and with Salvador's voice. When the song ended, I felt so sorry, so adrift. I felt melancholy. It was really strange. Salvador escorted me to my seat next to Rufina, who clapped softly. My heart was racing. I watched Salvador's long legs walking back to the patio as he called to Luis's fiancée, "Maria Elena, Maria Elena, this is our song. Let's dance." I didn't hear the song; I saw only Salvador in his white long-sleeved *guayabrera* dancing on the patio, throwing back his head to laugh, his white, even teeth gleaming.

It is sad to think that on the night we danced *la bamba*, Salvador's own heart was breaking. I did not know until many years after his brother died, on the day that was to be our wedding, that Salvador had loved Maria Elena from the time they were all children together. In the years following Luis's death, Salvador continued to hope that Maria Elena would agree to marry him. But she never did.

While I thought of these things, my Mamá Sofía had stopped crying. She was tracing a pattern on the oilcloth with her thumb. I thought of the doctor, and how she had tried to help me. I wanted to be well.

So I spoke softly, persuasively, to Mamá. "You could start planting vegetables again, Mamá Sofía. I could help you to get Papá into the hospital. We should leave, Mamá Sofía. The *milpas* around here are not good for us any more."

"Now that you are here, Luz Marina, maybe we can do the things you say, God willing."

Glancing at the letter again, I said, "Doña Catalina is planning to sell a lot of land."

"She has a lot to sell," Mamá Sofía said. "God, in his wisdom, continues to bless the Casal family. Of course they do some very good things. They are still assisting us, in a way, in spite of everything."

"Yes," I said, thinking of my children, feeling my lips tremble as I tried to smile. Mamá Sofía seemed slightly cheered to see me smile, for she said, "I know for sure Perla would help us more if she could, but her husband, as you know, is so stingy and proud. Then, I worry every minute about poor Concha and her family. They can hardly feed themselves."

"I'll talk to the pastor on Sunday, Mamá Sofía. In the meantime, rest a little. I'll see to Papá."

My mother gazed at me with a sad look on her face. "We'll see how he is. But don't be offended if he refuses your help."

I looked away quickly. I remembered the second time Salvador postponed our wedding, without any real reason. That night my parents advised me not to live with him, that he was unreliable. By then, I was pregnant with Feliciano, and could think of little but Salvador's wishes. I believed that Salvador would one day marry me, that he would be a good father, that he would protect me from harm, and from the poverty which threatened to engulf my family.

Later on, I reminded myself that Salvador was not the worst man in our area. Many of the men I knew had affairs and outside children. Salvador, in certain ways, was a typical man of San Joaquín, maybe in the whole of Belize, maybe in the world, for all I knew.

Until it began to happen, I never believed that he would rage at me when I tried to make some money through my sewing, that he would beat me if I didn't give him the money, lock us up, starve us, hate me. After a while, I could only speak with Salvador if he was in the mood to talk, which was less and less often.

My first Sunday morning at home was humid and overcast. I wandered around the outskirts of San Joaquín, reluctant to walk to the field where Pastor Felipe Rivas Ortega still held services under a huge tent. Nearby, the concrete church building was still under construction.

I walked along the dirt roads, listening to people's voices in the thatched houses. Pigs grunted in the mud, chickens fled squawking through yards, chased by mangy dogs, cows wandered about the fields and dirt roads. Fresh pats of dung were everywhere and I was careful to avoid soiling my shoes. This made me smile. The pastor would undoubtedly be thinking of the blot he imagined must be on my soul. He had visited me once in prison, urging me to confess my sins and be cleansed. I suppose he imagined himself walking beside me to the gallows, where at the time I had no intention of going if I could help it.

In the distance, smoke rose from cooking fires and burning *milpas*. Nearer, the acrid scent of scorched fields filled my nostrils. I smelt tortillas baking on iron griddles, and fresh coffee. The people I saw wore Sunday clothes, the men in white shirts and pants, sandals and straw hats, the women in skirts of red, green and yellow, and white embroidered blouses. Children walked beside them, subdued. Sundays were fairly quiet days, and people were on their way to the churches in the neighbourhood.

The streets seemed more crowded than I remembered; probably there were more newcomers from El Salvador or Guatemala. During my swim in the river the evening before, I saw people erecting thatched houses in the bushes.

I stood to the rear of the tent when I arrived. The service was half over and I was grateful for this. I saw many old friends there, but I kept my eyes on the grass beneath my feet, trying not to remember my children's shrieks of pain, and the repeated thuds of Salvador's leather belt.

I tried not to think about the cigarette burns on Feliciano's face. My eldest son always tried to protect us from his father. Salvador could not help himself, I know. To the end, we loved the Salvador we first knew. But I fought the later Salvador, our enemy, to the death, as it turned out.

When I was at Doña Catalina's, I had two days off every month. On about my twelfth or thirteenth visit to our *milpa*, Papá Apolonio said, "Luz Marina, you are truly a light." He rubbed his calloused hands over the top of my hair. He was seldom free from pain since his injuries at the last festival. I gave him the two bottles of aspirin I brought home each month.

"So, tell me, Papá Apolonio," I said, "how is the pain?"

"Ah, the same, the same," he said, dismissing my concern with a wave of his hand. "I am used to it now."

I looked at my parents with affection. They looked brighter, more hopeful. The money I was earning was making life easier for all of us.

Papá Apolonio was sitting near the doorway of our old home, smoking his pipe, "You'll never guess what has happened, Luz Marina."

"What?" I asked, going to stand beside him.

"Salvador Joaquín brought a new preacher to see us. He wanted to ask us to attend his church." He called to my mother who was cooking at the fire hearth. "Madre, what is the name of the new church?"

"Evangelica," Mamá Sofía said, turning a face that was eager and bright. "We enjoyed the service, Luz Marina."

"Papá," I said, "Salvador and Doña Catalina had a big fight over money one day. When it was time for mass, he wouldn't go with Doña Catalina. He said he was never going back to the Church of San Joaquín."

"He's joined Evangelica," Papá said. "He told me that he'd given up the gambling and the drinking."

"Salvador said that?"

"Oh yes. Members of Evangelica talk freely with one another."

Perla and Concha were around the wooden washing bowl in a far corner of the yard. Perla was washing their school uniforms and Concha was pinning the clothes on the line. It must have been the dry season for the day was sunny, breezy and cool.

"Papá Apolonio," I said sadly, "Salvador has left Doña Catalina's home. He lives in a small house by the river."

"Salvador knows what he is doing, I guess," Papá Apolonio said. "He and this new pastor have become good friends. Mamá Sofía and I have decided to join Evangelica."

"But what will the fathers at the Church of San Joaquín think of us? They married you, baptised us, and Concha and Perla go to school there."

"I suppose you are really worried about Doña Catalina's opinion, but I don't think there is any cause for worry. Salvador's money helped to start Evangelica."

I was silent.

"This new pastor believes that his prayers will perform a miracle. He will pray over me, and ask all his congregation to do the same at the service tomorrow night. He will put his hands on my feet, ask God to forgive my sins, and command the pain to stop."

"You believe this, Papá Apolonio?"

"I have to believe in the power of prayer, of course," Papá Apolonio said. "I want to try. You will join us at the service, Luz Marina?"

I nodded. If it comforted my parents to believe Papá Apolonio could be cured by prayer, perhaps it would happen.

"Evangelica raises money to help the sick and the crippled," Papá Apolonio was saying. "Remember the man who almost lost his eye when the horse kicked him? Evangelica sent him to doctors in America. His eye is almost as good as new now."

Several months passed. During that time, the new pastor and Salvador Joaquín made regular visits to my family's home on the *milpa*, and to the others living in the surrounding bush. The pastor and Salvador encouraged them to attend the services under the tent in the big field, which belonged to Doña Catalina and Don Pablo. "How can I refuse a request from God?" Doña Catalina replied, when I asked her about it. "Maybe God will help Salvador Joaquín. I can't."

In the meantime, the new pastor continued praying over Papá Apolonio in public and in private. Papá Apolonio began to say that the pain was almost entirely gone. But Mamá Sofía told me he was taking as many aspirins as he ever did.

At one of the services, Mamá Sofía and Papá Apolonio proclaimed their gratitude to God and to the pastor, and they became devoted members of the new church. In due course, the entire settlement of fifty men, women and children, following the example of my parents, abandoned their old faith and became a part of Pastor Felipe Rivas Ortega's congregation. They decided to raise funds to build a church.

The settlement came together in a spirit of community and good feeling. Neighbours decided, at least temporarily, to abandon their suspicions of each other. It was time, the pastor urged, to band together as a group. As a symbol of their new resolve, the members of Evangelica decided to give the settlement a name. At first so many names were suggested that a series of quarrels started again. Eventually they settled on the name of Esperanza, which means hope, and who could quarrel with hope?

At Evangelica, that first Sunday, it was hard for me to believe that I had been so long in prison, that I was once again listening to singing voices under this tent and that Salvador was gone. When the service was over, the congregation streamed out of the tent towards the tables of food and drink. Many people had walked quite a distance to reach Esperanza Evangelical Church. A few people, startled to see me, nodded in my direction and continued on their way.

I stood in line to shake the pastor's hand, and to say a few words to him. He was dressed in a dark suit, a shirt and tie; his wet hair was combed back from his forehead. His eyes were kindly under bushy, untidy eyebrows. He was of medium height and build, and stood with both hands extended as I approached.

"Good afternoon, pastor," I said, shaking his hand briefly. His face did not betray any surprise. He shook my hand vigorously and I could feel his ring biting into my flesh. His voice was heavy and hearty, pitched to the parishioners rather than to me.

"Welcome, Luz Marina. Glad you could join us today. Will you stay and have some *almuerzo*?"

"I was hoping to talk with you about serving the church, Pastor, and ask your help in finding a job."

"Of course. Join the ladies, you know most of them. I'll talk with you as soon as I can."

My hands were cold and clammy as I walked over to the long wooden table, covered with a white cloth. The leader of the women's group, Dolores Gonzalez Paz, was supervising the serving of food to the families who had attended the service. We had known each other as girls in school. She used to like me. The folds of her neck were caked with talcum powder mixed with sweat.

"Luz Marina? Girl, I didn't know you were home. Have you said hello to Pastor Ortega?"

"Yes. He suggested I wait for him here. How are you, Dolores?" We looked into each other's eyes.

"Big and fat as you see me, Luz Marina. I am still married. I had another daughter since I saw you last."

"How many children do you have now, Dolores?"

"Eight and they're eating us out of house and home! We've opened a shop near Plaza San Joaquín. But what's new with you?"

She leaned across the table and gave me a hug. Tears filled my eyes. She saw them. "My dear," she said, "such is life. What can we do? Give me a hand with this pot of stewed chicken."

As we lifted it on to the table, I asked, "But where is Tomás?" I remembered her husband as devoted to his family, and a very supportive member of Esperanza Evangelica.

"As to him, don't even ask. We had an argument just before I left home today." She handed me a stack of paper plates and a long-handled spoon.

"Really?" It was hard to imagine her husband, a handsome, heavyset man with curly black hair and a ready smile, arguing with anyone, let alone Dolores.

"He's joined something called the Belize Environmental Action Group which is taking up all his spare time. He wants me to go with him door to door getting signatures, and I'm already so busy."

"What for?"

"There's a rumour going around that a few big landowners in San Joaquín are planning to sell a vast amount of land to foreign buyers, but I can hardly believe it."

"Nor I, Dolores," I said, setting out the plates on the table.

As we began serving the food, she said, "I don't suppose it's illegal or anything like that. But it stands to reason that the government wouldn't want to lose control over so much of the country, don't you think?"

"That's true," I said. "People would have to move. Where would they go?"

It felt good to be in a conversation with an old friend. It had been so long since I'd spoken with anyone about anything other than my own difficulties. Perhaps she more than anyone else outside my family understood what my life with Salvador had been like. I could count on her not to mention his name unless I did.

"Exactly," Dolores said, spooning a piece of chicken on to a plate, while I added the salad and tortillas. "According to Tomás, everything would disappear." She waved a spoon vaguely in the direction of the hills and jungle behind her.

"Impossible," I said, hoping she would continue to talk. Her voice had always had a settling effect on me.

"Not according to my learned husband. He said profit is what big landowners think about, not people's livelihood, let alone the Río Caracol, and certainly not jungle, animals and birds."

"How about the ruins?" I couldn't imagine them disappearing.

"Forget about it," Dolores said, "according to Tomás. Of course, he thinks the whole of Belize is his personal business, but I beg to respectfully disagree, as I told him."

I found myself smiling at the indignation on her face, red and round, as she recounted the lively conversation in her household.

"You see," Dolores said, passing me a plate of food, "I can still make you smile with my nonsense, which is all it is, I hope. Tomás is sometimes too energetic for his own good."

When the crowd at the table began thinning out, Dolores said to me, "Things are slowing down here. Could you walk around with these barbecue tickets? Evangelica is still trying to raise funds for the church building."

I nodded and she gave me five tickets in an envelope, just as the pastor arrived, rubbing his hands in anticipation of the food which Dolores Gonzalez Paz placed into his hands.

"Sit, Luz Marina," he said, motioning to the chairs scattered on the grass. "So what can we do for you?"

I again explained my need to do community service through the church, and that I needed to find a job and a place to live. He nodded, as if my needs were not a surprise.

"I'm glad you visited the church so soon. I'll mention that in my report to your probation officer. But why do you want to move from your house, with your father ill and your mother not much better, I expect?"

I handed him the letter which Ducho had delivered.

"Ah," he said, as he read it. "Ah." He folded the letter and returned it to me without comment. After a while, he said, "You remember Elodio Alpuche Guerra? He doesn't belong to our congregation, of course, but, like Doña Catalina, he makes a generous contribution every now and then."

I nodded, wondering what Elodio would think of me.

"He was saying only last week when I visited his office that he needs someone to assist his secretary for a few weeks. He might be willing to hire you. A place to live for your family might be more difficult. Let me see what can be done."

"Thank you, Pastor."

"Oh, don't think about it. You worked hard for the church in the past, as I remember."

"Yes," I said, sensing he was becoming uncomfortable as our conversation strayed near the subject of Salvador.

"Well, I must talk with some other people, but we are so happy to have you back. I hope to see you often." He turned to Dolores Gonzalez Paz.

"Talk to Luz Marina about joining your group, please, Dolores? You'll find her diligent in whatever she does."

"Yes, of course, Pastor," Dolores said, beckoning me to rejoin her at the table. "We still meet every Thursday evening. The next meeting is at my house. Can you come?"

"Yes, thank you."

"*Nada, nada*," she said. She was about to pat my shoulder, thought better of it and said, "See if you can sell the tickets."

I wandered around, feeling disoriented and as dull as the sky overhead, my limbs heavy. I felt a great need to sleep, only I couldn't sleep. My nights were disturbing, not only from the sounds my father made, and my mother's frequent trips to his hammock, but from my own thoughts. There was nowhere I could go where it was quiet and clean and bright.

I picked up my courage and approached groups of people I didn't know offering them the tickets, but nobody wanted to buy any. I didn't want to give up so soon, so I continued to circle the grounds, the pink cardboard tickets in my hand. Salvador and Papá Apolonio had been among the pastor's first converts, and the congregation elected them to head the fundraising drive. Salvador knew a lot of rich and important people in the town of San Joaquín, and Papá Apolonio knew all of the *milperos*. Between them, quite a lot of money was collected for the church building.

In those days, whenever I was at home, I attended the new church with Mamá Sofía, Papá Apolonio, Perla and Concha. Within a few months, Papá Apolonio seemed much better. It felt good to see him so self-respecting again, so important in Esperanza Evangelica. The pastor assigned Papá Apolonio to visit certain homes every week.

After a few months, Papá Apolonio began talking to people about God's word, and reading to them marked passages in the Bible, as he had been taught to do by the new pastor. Whenever he met new people from across the border, he told them about Esperanza Evangelica.

Whether it was the regular exercise, or the pastor's prayers, Papá Apolonio began taking fewer and fewer aspirins. Sometimes on Sundays, the five of us walked about the settlement together, carrying Bibles and leaflets.

As I wandered now about the grounds of Esperanza Evangelica, the tickets in my hand, the sky turned from a hazy blue to a bright orange. People drifted towards their homes, carrying tables, chairs, pots, pans and other containers lent for the occasion.

When even Pastor Rivas Ortega had driven away in his truck, I hurried to where Dolores was still busy at the tables; paper plates and remnants of food filled the drums near the entryway. I helped Dolores and other women to scrub pots and pans with pumblestones, and with coconut trash pulled from the husks littering the edges of the field.

As I returned home that evening, I tried not to remember that for several years, so it seems, Salvador did not always turn in to the church leaders all the money he collected from donors. The pastor was very disappointed when he discovered this. No charges were pressed against Salvador because the pastor had been his friend. Salvador did not return to Esperanza Evangelica, and then neither could the children and I.

On Monday afternoon, we were very surprised when the pastor drove up to our door. He told Mamá Sofía and me that I was to report to Elodio Alpuche Guerra's office the following day for an interview. After the pastor left, Mamá Sofía and I could not feel as simply thankful as we should have done. We felt somehow disloyal as we remembered Papá Apolonio's fight with José Alpuche Guerra at the festival several years before.

The next morning, I arrived at the office of Elodio Alpuche Guerra. It was the day of his daughter's *quince años*, and the office was decorated with birthday balloons and streamers. The servants were out in the grounds setting out tables and chairs for his daughter's fifteenth birthday celebration later that day.

Elodio Alpuche Guerra was now a large, fleshy man of about thirty-five years of age, only a year or two older than I. His eyes were small and very black, and he spoke very softly. Mamá Sofía had told me that he had become wealthy through land deals. He owned several large grocery stores in three of the six districts in the country. He also had an import-export commission agency. With his money, he bought a large estate with a beautiful house. Mamá Sofía said that he had become very powerful, and very influential with the politicians in San Joaquín.

Señor Elodio, as I heard people refer to him, was in a good mood. Straight away I could tell that he had no memory of ever having given me a golden chain with a cross when we were teenagers. He sat behind his desk in a black swivel chair facing a huge window, through which he could see his home, a portion of his estate, cattle and horses.

His secretary, Rosa Christina, and his personal assistant, Pedro Fernandez, were seated in the large room, when I was shown in by the messenger. I had spent another sleepless night, anxious about this interview, wondering if he would ask about Salvador, the trial and my probation. But he didn't. In a way I was very grateful that he treated me much as he would a stranger.

"So, Miss Figueroa," he said, "I will ask you to help my secretary for a few weeks until her ankle is better." He rose, selected a bag of sweets tied with ribbons from a basket on his desk, and gave it to me with a grave politeness.

"My daughter is fifteen years old today, almost a woman. I hope you will accept this small gift from her."

Taking the bag, I said, "With pleasure, Señor Elodio. I wish your daughter all that I wish my own."

We shook hands and, before I had left the room, he and his assistant had returned to the papers strewn across his desk.

The following Monday I arrived punctually at nine o'clock and assisted Rosa Christina with the filing, and with carrying trays of food and drink to the large number of people who visited the office. Rosa had twisted her ankle badly jumping out of a van on to the gravel driveway leading to the front door of the building. She managed to get around on crutches, but I did most of the fetching and carrying for her.

"I hate staying at home, Luz Marina," she told me. "You cannot imagine how boring it is for me, listening to my mother and her sisters. My Tía Marta says I am a lousy wife and mother!"

There was laughter in her eyes, so I smiled.

"Oh, I admit my shortcomings freely when I am at home, Luz Marina. It's the best way, don't you agree?"

I felt my face redden; tears filled my eyes. She passed me a tissue from the box on her desk. "We are a fine pair, you and I, but I think we will work well together?"

"Oh yes, Rosa Christina, I am sure we will."

I worked each weekday in the office, and was soon helping Rosa to prepare for a big meeting. It was to take place one Monday about six weeks after I'd started to work there.

The morning of the meeting was hot and humid, with brief showers that left the air more uncomfortable than it had been before. Tension was high in the office and we worked almost in silence.

The hum of the fans was loud and outside the window white birds seemed to float on the backs of black cows. In the distance, the stones of a cemetery on the edge of a field stood out sharply, casting shadows on the grass. Colourful wreaths, made from crêpe paper twisted around wire, were heaped on a fresh mound. I suddenly wished I could take flowers to Salvador's grave but this was not possible. Doña Catalina's lands were out of bounds to me.

At ten o'clock landowners and other business people began arriving. I had no idea what the meeting was about, but I knew it was very important, as among those invited were a number of foreigners. Perhaps they were from the United States, Canada or England.

Rosa had typed the agenda for the meeting and photocopied it herself. She asked Pedro to place the copies on the long table, which seated twelve, in the middle of the glassed-in veranda converted to a conference room.

My small desk was situated in a corner of Rosa's office, near the filing cabinets, copying machine and the door to the kitchen where a cook served both the household and the office. Today she was going to serve sandwiches, juice, coffee and biscuits at lunchtime.

All the previous week Señor Elodio had spent hours on the telephone. Many faxes and cables arrived from abroad. Rosa had no time to join me for coffee breaks. She hobbled back and forth across the room to a locked filing cabinet in Señor Elodio's office.

By about ten-thirty the meeting had started. Every now and then there was a sudden burst of laughter and then the voices subsided again to a low murmur.

The meeting must have gone well, for people left laughing and talking amiably to each other. Señor Elodio returned to the office accompanied by two men, one of whom was Andrés, Doña Catalina's second son. My hands became cold.

Unlike Salvador who, in the early days, used to sometimes compliment me openly to annoy Doña Catalina, Andrés tried to flatter me whenever there was no one around to hear him. I believed he envied Salvador's good looks and popularity, and tried to outdistance him in any way he could.

In those days I sometimes found Andrés's efforts at flirtation a little comical and laughed to myself when he wasn't looking. However, the night I found him in my room reading a book in my bed, I returned to the kitchen and began helping Rufina to squeeze oranges for Sunday's breakfast.

Salvador had been away for several days and I was frightened that Andrés would suggest to him on his return that we had become lovers. As I emptied a sack of oranges into the sink and turned on the tap, Rufina said, "It's nearly midnight." She was thinking, I knew, that I had to be ready before six the following day to attend mass with Doña Catalina. I shrugged, scrubbing the dirt off a green-skinned orange. I wiped my face with the sleeve of my dress.

"Are you sick?" Rufina asked.

I shook my head, making a sudden decision. "Andrés is reading in my bed," I said.

"Si?" Rufina asked, her narrow black eyes sharpening as she carefully examined my face. I thought of the night, more than a year before, when I was fifteen and she had plaited sweet-smelling jasmine into my hair.

I nodded, allowing my hair to fall forward, covering my face. Rufina wiped her hands on her apron and stepped out into the corridor. She pushed the door of my room and stepped inside. After a minute or two I heard Andrés laughing and talking with Rufina in the corridor. On her return to the kitchen, she said, "Go to bed, Luz Marina. Lock your door when you are in your room, and whenever you leave it. It's for the best."

My bedroom at Doña Catalina's was very precious to me. The walls were painted a bright blue, and the mosquito netting was tied above an iron bed. I had a little night table, a chest of drawers and a wardrobe. The ceiling and shutters were white. The polished wooden floor was bare, except for a woven mat next to the bed.

On my return there from the kitchen that night, I stared at the indentation of Andrés's body on my pillow and on the white chenille bedspread with the blue fringe. The scent of his aftershave lingered in the air. I opened the windows, and leaned my forehead against the screen listening to the crying crickets and the barking of the dogs far away.

Elodio Alpuche Guerra seemed not to have remembered that I was in the office, for he stood near Rosa's desk talking with Andrés Casal and the other man, who I soon realised was a local politician.

They were obviously pleased with the way the meeting had gone for they were laughing and joking. All at once I heard Andrés say, "My family is all for it. Join the team, Elodio." Andrés had the same booming voice as his father, Don Pablo.

"I don't know," Elodio Alpuche Guerra said. "I'll wait to see how things go before I commit myself. It is a lot of money, of course."

"If you hold out, others will too, and on our own we won't have the needed acreage to sell. It's a once in a lifetime deal," Andrés replied.

Although I could not see him, I knew that he was probably rocking back and forth on his heels, as he always liked to do. His hands were probably in his pockets, his teeth bared in a grin he did not mean.

"True," Elodio Alpuche Guerra said. "But I don't know how I feel about foreigners owning that much land around here, Andrés. Give me some time on this, eh?"

"How much?" Andrés laughed.

"I don't know, but I don't want a lot of pressure. I'm set up here now and I like it." Elodio Alpuche Guerra's soft voice began to sound strained.

"What do you mean by pressure, man?" Andrés's voice became even more playful.

"Well, I'm beginning to feel that your family, the other owners and Miguel Rivas here, are in too big a hurry to sell. Some people in the country, and in the government, are not going to like it."

"You know how to make your way through the House of Representatives, don't you, Miguel?"

"I believe so," the politician replied. "If there is enough to go around. Don't forget I am responsible for the welfare of a few public servants as well as my constituents."

"There'll be enough," Andrés said. "When is the next meeting, by the way?"

They drifted towards Elodio Alpuche Guerra's office and I was greatly relieved that Andrés had not noticed me. I couldn't believe it. "Luz Marina," I said to myself, "that was good luck. Please put your head on the pillow in the same place as last night."

Rosa and I became busy, and I thought no more of what I had overheard. But later that day, Elodio Alpuche Guerra came to my desk and said, "Miss Figueroa, the pastor tells me that you need to move from where you are living now."

I always wondered about Elodio Alpuche Guerra. Whenever he looked at me, he kept all signs of recognition from his eyes. But men are sometimes like that. Take Salvador – often he claimed he could not recall conversations we had from one week to the next, or even one day to the next.

"Yes, Señor Elodio," I said, not looking up at him. "The land is going to be sold."

"Who owns it?" I could tell he was still uneasy about his conversation with Andrés.

"I think the Casal family." I tried to say the name as casually as I could.

He stood for a moment, looking through the window at several brown horses galloping across the field. I wondered if he was thinking, as I was, of that long-ago festival when his father, José Alpuche Guerra, and my Papá Apolonio had the fight. I longed to talk about that terrifying night. But if I mentioned it to Señor Elodio, he would probably look at me sideways, the way Salvador used to do, and say, "I don't recall that, no."

"I'm sorry your family is going through these difficulties," Señor Elodio said. "There are two empty rooms in the quarters behind our house. It's not a home exactly, but it might do until you can find someplace else to live. There will be no charge."

"Thank you, Señor Elodio," I said, keeping my voice steady, emotionless. But I was thinking that it had been such a lucky day for me. I felt so good, but I controlled my sense of elation. I remembered how Salvador used to tell me, "You are so easily pleased, Luz Marina." His voice always held a tinge of scorn whenever he said that, so I knew it was not a compliment.

"Oh, it is as nothing. I'll tell Pedro Fernandez to get it prepared, put in some furniture. The rooms are a good size."

"Thank you, Señor."

"It's nothing, nothing. You work well and I would like you to be comfortable. We work together here in a confidential manner, you know?"

"I understand," I replied.

As we drank coffee during our break, Rosa Christina told me that Señor Elodio was deeply in love with his wife, a pretty, gentle woman, who was the mother of his three sons and three daughters. It pained me to listen to Rosa talk about the blessings of the Elodio Alpuche Guerra home. It was envy, I know. *Ay, Dios.*

I stared into her soft brown eyes, smiled, drank the second cup of coffee she gave to me and tried to concentrate instead on my Papá Apolonio. I wondered if he would understand why I was planning to bring him to live on the property of Elodio Alpuche Guerra, the eldest son of his old friend, turned enemy, José Alpuche Guerra.

I was purposely late the evening of the church barbecue. It rained for about two hours in the early afternoon. I waited to dress, hoping that the downpour would continue and then the barbecue would have to be cancelled. But the rain stopped about five, and by the time I arrived at the church grounds it was nearly dark. I was glad, trusting that nobody would notice as I slipped behind the table and began helping Dolores Gonzalez Paz and the others to put meat on the grill.

The sale of tickets had gone well, I was glad to see. Hundreds of adults and children moved about the grounds, which were transformed by hurricane lamps, Chinese lanterns and fairy lights. As usual my stomach was churning with anxiety, and I was suddenly exhausted. Perhaps it was partly caused by the voices of so many children running in and out of the crowd. I thought I heard Teresa shout, "Mamá!", but when I turned round it was another little girl. Still, I continued to scour the faces of the children there, hoping to see the beloved faces of my own.

My need to be with Feliciano, Teresa and Eduardo makes me drift like a ghost through Doña Catalina's home for most of each night. Even as I rise from my hammock to assist Mamá Sofía with Papá Apolonio, I ask myself silly questions like whether or not I really watered more than fifty house plants each week. Is the glittering chandelier, above the shining mahogany dining table and ten chairs, as large and bright as I seem to remember?

Does Doña Catalina tell my children, as she did me, that the prints on the enormous red and black carpet are the shape of elephants' feet? I feel sure that my children must sleep in the bedrooms that once belonged to Salvador, Andrés and Luis. And when exactly did Doña Catalina stop inviting me to sit with her on the *galeria*?

The sight of the buckets of chicken entrails, feathers and blood to the rear of the red-hot grills is almost more than I can bear. The marimba music is disturbing to me as it brings back memories and thoughts of happier nights when Salvador and I strolled through the plaza together. When did I seem to become indifferent to Doña Catalina's displeasure?

Although my relationship with Salvador ended almost a year before his death, I can hardly breathe whenever anything causes me to think of him, or of the night he died. The anger churns away inside me day after day. I argue with him endlessly in my mind even though I realise that during those last months he had been very ill, over the edge, and could not help himself.

"Why, Salvador," I ask him in my mind, "did you defy the court order to stay away from us over and over again? Why didn't you consult a doctor like we begged you to do?"

There are no answers, of course, to my questions. In San Joaquín we believe that there is life after death in a world of spirits. However, Salvador thought that was a ridiculous idea so I can't imagine where he can be at this moment.

If he were here with me at the barbecue, Salvador would say that I am driving him mad, repeating the same questions over and over again. Right at this moment I am trying to consider changing my name from Luz Marina to one like Dolores. People would call me Dolor, Dully, or perhaps Dullita, and I would hear a good, solid thud in my ears, instead of seeing a flash of light across the sea whenever people call my name.

It was so hard for me to see then, although I certainly understand very well now, how Salvador could look so well on the outside and yet be so ill on the inside. He was either frantically busy or so depressed he could hardly manage to get out of bed in the mornings. Perhaps I should not have pretended that I didn't notice. But by then I had become very much afraid of his rages, not only for myself but for Feliciano, Teresa and Eduardo.

As I turned the pieces of chicken sizzling on the huge barbecue at Esperanza Evangelica, I thought of my old church of San Joaquín. I thought of the candles, the pictures of the saints, and the holy water. Best of all to me was the anonymity and the lack of demands made on me by the priests there. I wanted to go back, even though it meant walking two miles to San Joaquín like I used to do when I sold *tamales* in the plaza.

Several things stopped me. The pastor and people of the Esperanza Evangelical Church accepted me, in spite of my sin, "into the fold", as the pastor said. Whatever they might think or say about me behind my back, in front of my face they treated me like a sinner who has returned to God.

At the San Joaquín Church, I might come face to face with Doña Catalina. She would be merciless. I would need to face her one day, but I wanted to be strong enough then to be able to say, "Give my children back to me, Doña Catalina, or a court order will be served against you." How I loved the sound of those words. At the Church of San Joaquín, I might meet the old priest who confirmed me. He would ask me, I felt sure, "Have you been to confession as yet, Luz Marina?" I have asked God for His forgiveness, but I am not sure what I would confess to anyone.

I also have to admit to myself that I don't feel well enough to walk to San Joaquín in the hot sun.

The house in which we now live leaks whenever it rains. Some of the hinges are off the windows, a number of panes are broken and covered with old Belize City newspapers. Everything inside the house seems to be falling apart. Outside, the bush has grown thick and close, choking the banana suckers and other plants. I nervously scurry up the path at night, whenever the services at church keep me from getting home before dark. Why I should be afraid, after what I have done, puzzles me.

The doctor has told me to use my reason, but right now it seems I don't have any. We had an argument about ghosts during my last visit. She claims she does not believe in spirits and ghosts. The doctor can get me to believe almost anything, except that.

I cannot wait for the end of August when we will be moving into the rooms belonging to Elodio Alpuche Guerra, although the thought that I am perhaps betraying my Papá Apolonio makes my head ache as well.

My one consolation is that my mother seems relieved to be finally leaving Casal precincts. "Papá Apolonio is beyond caring what happens to him, Luz Marina, or to us," she said to me when I told her about Elodio Alpuche Guerra's offer. "How can we be too proud to accept his kindness? And he is a kind man, that we know. May he always prosper."

I am working here on the fields of Evangelica because I am grateful for the practical help the pastor is giving to us. Earlier today, as we were setting out the barbecue tables and chairs, he promised, without my having to ask, to have members of the men's group transport my father to Elodio Alpuche Guerra's *rancho*. I am looking forward to living on it.

Perhaps the neatly thatched whitewashed buildings, the cleared paths, the open fields, the daily routine of going to work and returning to a new home, will ease our pain and guilt. I don't know. I am hoping.

As I place tortillas, chicken and beans on paper plates, I wonder about this terrible anger I still feel towards Salvador, and what I can do to change these feelings which are overpowering. They are holding me back, shutting out people who would like to help me, to be kind like Rosa Christina at the office and Dolores Gonzalez Paz here.

I need friends to console me sometimes in the midst of enemies like Doña Catalina and her family. Even Rufina keeps her distance, fearing the wrath of the Casal family. I don't blame her of course. Still, I had hoped she would send me a message of some kind about my Feliciano, Teresa and Eduardo.

I was thinking of them so hard that I thought I was imagining things when I looked up to pass along two filled plates. I saw Doña Catalina talking with a group of people in the middle of the field. I noticed that Elodio Alpuche Guerra stood with them and my heart started beating rapidly. I wondered what she was doing here but, when Andrés joined them, my heart slowed down. The Casals were discussing their business deals, I felt sure. I began thinking of the conversation I'd heard in the office.

Perhaps this is what caused me to start babbling to the woman who was working beside me. She was laughing and joking with people who kept coming to the table with tickets for food. I knew Luisa Valles Flores did not like me, had never liked me, but in my nervousness and anxiety I said to her, "People are still streaming in. What a lot of tickets we sold." As soon as I said this I could have bitten off my tongue for I hadn't sold any tickets.

Luisa Valles glanced at me derisively, then agreed. She continued smiling and chatting to people as though she was waging a political campaign, and every vote counted. What forced me to open my mouth again, I will never know, but I said, "Did you sell any tickets? I tried but I couldn't. I'm so sorry about that."

"Oh, don't worry, Luz Marina. We had good fortune on the Saturday we went to Plaza San Joaquín. By chance we met Doña Catalina going for a stroll with her darling grandchildren. She bought twenty-five tickets." She glanced at me again, her eyes gleeful, so it seemed to me.

Blood rushed to my face. I tried to use caution. I gave myself strict instructions to be silent.

"You know how she loves to walk and talk with people she meets. Such a humble lady for somebody so important and rich."

"Yes," I said, thinking of Teresa and Eduardo out for a stroll in the plaza. Feliciano, although he is the eldest, would have been in his crib, which prevents him from falling out of bed. He has been in a coma for over two years. I am sure Rufina must have stayed with him.

On a day when Salvador was in a good mood, he took Feliciano horseback riding in the Mountain Pine Ridge. Feliciano liked horses but he was afraid of them. He didn't want to go but Salvador said, "You're getting to be too much of a mamá's boy."

According to the story Salvador told me, the horse was going very fast and Feliciano fell, hitting his head against a rock. I thought of my wedding dress that drowned in the Río Caracol, and couldn't believe that he had told me exactly what had happened. While Feliciano was in hospital, I packed the children's things and one night, when Salvador was away, we left his house by the river, for a second time, to live with Mamá Sofía and Papá Apolonio.

We stayed with my parents for several months but then we returned to Salvador, who seemed so sorry for his actions. He flew with Feliciano to Mérida, Guatemala City and Houston in the United States trying to get help for him. But up to now Feliciano has not been able to wake up. He needs special, expensive care, which I am sure he gets in Doña Catalina's home.

"She is so anxious about your welfare, Luz Marina," Luisa was saying. "I was happy to be able to tell her that our pastor has found you a job with Señor Elodio Alpuche Guerra, and a place to live on his *rancho*."

I heard my own voice under the laughter and talking of people surging good-naturedly around the tables. "Doña Catalina is selling the land. That's why we have to move."

"Can you blame the poor Doña after what happened there?" She stopped, and then placed a tiny jewelled hand briefly on my own. "But, of course, who knows what happened there? Forgive me. We all welcome you back to our church."

But I knew she didn't welcome me. She had always wanted to be elected leader of the women's group instead of Dolores Gonzalez Paz to whom Salvador and I had given our support in the past. Luisa Valles had always envied the special status I had in the church when Salvador worked with the pastor. In her view, I hadn't done much to deserve so much consideration.

Anger kept bubbling up inside me and I said, "It's not because of what did or did not happen on the *milpa* that the Casals are selling the property, Luisa Valles. Doña Catalina and her family are never sentimental when it comes to money. I have that on good authority."

The ferocity in my voice was so terrible that Luisa stepped back quickly, spilling the hot beans on her sandals.

"Sorry, sorry," I said, bending down to wipe them from her feet, noting the delicacy and precision with which her toenails were cut, and the pearly pink nail polish adorning them.

I was truly sorry but Luisa moved her foot away from my hand, a stiff smile on her face. I passed her a glass of water which she poured over her feet. Why I was anxious to placate her, to win her friendship, to explain myself, I didn't know. I couldn't stop talking.

"It's not because of Salvador, Luisa. It's because they are getting a good price from a foreign company."

"Crazy, Luz Marina, you are crazy. You've always got every story wrong ever since we were girls in primary school. Remember that time when you told Sister Mary Jocasta that you saw me put a stick of chalk in my schoolbag? That was a lie."

"I am not crazy."

She shrugged, sucking her teeth. "I know for a fact that all this everlasting jungle will be burned to create electricity. That's why they are buying the land. People from San Joaquín, not foreigners, are going to build a factory so everyone can have cheap electricity."

"I am not crazy," I repeated, but she did not look at me. She continued ladling food on to the paper plates. "Take it back, Luisa."

She laughed and said, "Let's have a drink and forget about it. Aren't you thirsty?"

I nodded. "You've always got the story right, Luisa, ever since we were little." I tried to remember if I had seen her put chalk in her bag. I felt certain I had. But for the past twenty months of my life reality often seemed like unreality. I was not sure of very much any more.

"I for one will be glad for the electricity," she continued, opening two bottles of orange soda. She passed one to me. "Then I'll be able to sew in the evenings. Doña Catalina told me about this herself. She wanted to know what I thought of the idea."

That night, as we were saying goodbye to each other, Dolores Gonzalez Paz hugged Luisa Valles Flores, kissing her on both cheeks, and congratulating her on the fine ticket sales. After Luisa had disappeared in the crowd surging towards the gates, Dolores Paz said to me, "I saw you talking to Luisa, that snake in the grass. I hope you didn't tell her any of your business. Don't trust her."

"She got on my nerves, Dolores."

"Luisa gets on everybody's nerves. You of all people should know that. See you on Thursday."

"Yes," I said feeling very low, deciding to stay clear of Luisa Valles Flores in the future. What would Elodio Alpuche Guerra say or do if he ever heard I had carried news out of the office? He would be so disappointed in me. I had let myself down, and his mother would be bound to say, "Your heart is too soft, Elodio. What did you expect? Like father, like daughter, no?"

But weeks passed. We moved to Elodio Alpuche Guerra's *rancho*, and settled into our rooms, and a new routine. Eventually, the barbecue and Luisa Valles Flores receded to the back of my mind, and I settled down at work, hoping to be hired permanently. Rosa Christina's ankle was better by now, but she told me she was pregnant with her third child. It was quite likely Elodio Alpuche Guerra would keep me on.

One afternoon she said, "So how come you didn't tell me that you and Señor Elodio were boyfriend and girlfriend when you were young? You are so secretive, Luz Marina. My mother told me the whole story."

"I didn't mean to be secretive. Papá Apolonio and Señor Elodio's father had a big fight once, but that was, oh, long ago. I was trying ..."

"To be discreet, to be correct. I understand. I am the same way. It's not good to talk too much, to let everybody know your business, especially in San Joaquín."

Immediately I thought of Luisa Valles Flores. How could I have said what I had? Still, I know from my experience with

Salvador that some people can cause you to say and do the most unlikely things. I wish I knew why that was.

The hurricane season arrived, a time of the year everyone dreads. Thirty years ago was the last time we had a really bad storm, God be praised. However, a tropical depression had settled in the skies above us and it had been raining for days. I arrived at the office one Monday, soaking wet after a fifteen-minute walk across Elodio Alpuche Guerra's estate. Rosa looked harried, upset.

"An emergency meeting has been called for this afternoon at three o'clock, Luz Marina."

"What kind of meeting? What do you want me to do?" I looked anxiously at her face. She was pale, and her eyes looked reproachful.

"There is no agenda, or anything very much to do. I can handle what there is."

I sat down at my desk, rubbing my hand across the surface of smooth blond mahogany. I valued my place here, a link, however mysterious, to a better time in my life. The heavy downpour slowed to a drizzle. Sunlight filtered through the rain. The electric lights were on. For the rest of the morning, I concentrated on the filing in the wire baskets which Rosa had filled. She was not much of a talker in the mornings, but today she was absolutely silent as she typed steadily.

We ate our lunch at our desks, since it was too wet to go outdoors, as we sometimes did. Elodio Alpuche Guerra usually started work in his office at an unknown hour before we arrived. He usually left the office at ten or eleven to drive around the estate with the workers.

This morning, as he was going through the door, he said a curt good morning, without laughing and joking with us, which was surprising. He seemed not even to see me; this sent a chill through my body. During the afternoon, I was not asked to do any photocopying. Rosa opened the mail herself, so I kept on working. I felt dizzy with apprehension and could hardly see what I was doing.

By the time the doors of the cars, vans and trucks began to slam outside the patio of the cement block building, I'd managed to complete the day's filing, but decided to check to see if I'd done it correctly. I had nothing else to do.

By now, I knew which landowners were probably seated at the rectangular table on the patio. Pedro Fernandez had closed the windows and doors there against the weather. He had turned on the lights and fans, placed water in a pitcher and carried a tray to the elegant table in a corner where Rosa had placed a floral arrangement.

She, I knew, was now sitting in one corner of the room, waiting to take notes. It was odd not having anything specific to do and I felt restless, then increasingly uneasy. Each morning I looked forward to working in the busy, easygoing office. And life at home was getting better for us too.

Although we lived in only two connecting rooms, they were large and comfortable. Papá Apolonio's condition seemed no worse although more and more I got the feeling that he didn't quite know where he was most of the time. I have learned to be grateful for small mercies, as people like to say.

My mother and I had started a small business, nothing much. We baked bread and buns in huge black iron pots on the fire hearth to the rear of our rooms. Our customers were the workers on the estate, and the office workers, including Rosa Christina and Pedro Fernandez.

Mamá Sofía and I always had a lot to do, and to talk about. We had begun to send a few dollars to Concha who lived across the border in a Guatemalan village, and to save a little for ourselves. Perla continued to write, telling us to expect her at any time. She lived to the north, near the Mexican border.

Mamá Sofía still had her old sewing machine and I had begun making festival costumes again. When I had made a number of them, I would walk to the plaza, going from shop to shop, until I had sold them all. I planned to go at night when I could sit on one of the benches in the plaza across from Doña Catalina's home. At some point in the evening, Teresa and Eduardo might play on the *galeria*, especially when the weather was hot.

From October to March, a lot of tourists come to our area, and the local hotels are full then. They buy costumes too. This work, and caring for Papá Apolonio, kept Mamá Sofía and me busy almost every evening. We didn't discuss the dreadful memories that were almost always with us as we went about our various activities.

A worker from Elodio Alpuche Guerra's kitchen passed my desk with a coffee pot and mugs on a tray. On his return to the main office, I was surprised to see Rosa Christina come out behind him. Her face was a pasty white and she looked at me with worried eyes.

"Luz," she said, "you are needed in the meeting."

"For what?" I asked, alarmed. But I thought I knew, and feared, what it was going to be about.

"There is some problem with the Belize City newspapers." She went into Elodio Alpuche Guerra's office, and the door closed. I was to go in alone.

I stepped into the conference room on the patio, which seemed like a strange place with all the visitors seated around the gleaming table. Rosa had cleared it of all files and papers. Señor Elodio sat at the head of the table, and next to him was Pedro, his assistant.

I moved my eyes slowly over the faces looking at me. My eyes met Doña Catalina's and my heart jumped. I had expected to see Andrés. So far, there had been only two moments in my life worse than this: the day when the doctors told Salvador and me that Feliciano might never emerge from his coma, and the night Salvador died. I looked around the room, wondering why Doña Catalina was there without Andrés.

I noticed Doña Catalina's smart business suit, a pale mauve, her diamond jewellery sparkling in her ears, at her throat and on her fingers. As usual her fingernails were exquisitely manicured.

"Sit down, please, Luz Marina," Señor Elodio said to me. His voice sounded hoarse. Pedro pulled out a chair. I sat down, folded my hands in my lap, and kept my eyes on the newspapers in the centre of the table. There were several.

Señor Elodio picked up the one in front of him. He shook it open to the middle page, where his picture stared up at him. Beside it was one of Doña Catalina Casal.

"There's an anonymous article in this newspaper, and in one or two of the others, that talks about a large land sale to a foreign company by several of us seated here. The article exaggerates, of course, but it has enough facts to give us concern."

I must have had a blank look on my face for he continued, "It says that word about this has been leaked to the press by a woman recently employed by myself. It also mentions another business venture, a factory which would require the burning of six thousand acres of jungle annually to produce cheaper electricity."

My eyes flashed to Doña Catalina, who sat at the opposite end of the table. She was staring at the papers beneath her hands, as if waiting for a private conversation to end.

"Do you know anything about this, Luz Marina? Have you spoken to anyone about what you may have learnt here?"

I nodded, explaining as best as I could what had occurred the night of the church barbecue. When I mentioned what Luisa Valles Flores had said to me, Doña Catalina immediately held up her hand.

"Please leave my name out of this conversation," she said. "I absolutely deny ever discussing these matters with Luisa Valles Flores."

Señor Elodio looked very upset. His face reddened and he took several sips of water.

"I don't know what made me say the things I did that night, Señor Elodio. I am sorry."

Nodding in my direction, but without looking at me, he said, "That will be all. Thank you."

I sat at my desk in silence waiting for five o'clock. Pedro usually gave us all a ride home around that time. The downpour had started again. Rosa Christina typed and typed.

When the meeting ended Señor Elodio said to me before entering his office, "The filing is all caught up now, Rosa tells me. We won't be needing your services after today. You may stay in the rooms until you find another place to stay – let us say in two weeks' time? Please give my best wishes to your family."

Rosa handed me an envelope, which must have been prepared earlier that day. "The cheque inside is generous, Luz Marina. I will miss you. Pedro! Give Luz Marina a ride home. Can't you see it is raining?"

"I don't need a ride, thank you Rosa," I said, retrieving my umbrella from the rear of the filing cabinet. I had caused Señor Elodio enough trouble. In Belize City, the lawyer would have seen the newspapers. He and his wife would probably be disappointed in me. I was disappointed in myself. I walked across the pastures to our rooms, not noticing the rain, conscious only of an inner chill, a feeling of intense fear. Doña Catalina had lied, I felt sure.

I pushed open the door to our rooms and knew at once that Papá Apolonio's condition must be worse, for a nurse was bending over him as he lay in bed. She was giving him an injection.

"How is he, Nurse Pineda?" Mamá Sofía asked, her voice tremulous.

"He should be in hospital," the nurse said, easing her bulk into a sagging armchair near Papá Apolonio's bed. She fanned her sweating face with a large handkerchief.

"My husband is so afraid of hospitals," Mamá Sofía said, "but if you think it would help him, we will do it."

"Who knows?" the nurse said. "But you should try. He's not responding to our help any more."

"Then we'll take him," my mother said. "Ah, Luz Marina, you are here. Papá is going down."

"I'll send the ambulance," the nurse said, "You never know, sometimes the heart is stronger than we think it is."

At the San Joaquín Hospital that night, we sat in the corridor outside Papá Apolonio's ward praying for his recovery. I told Mamá Sofía what had happened at Elodio Alpuche Guerra's office earlier that day. Our burdens were heavy that night. I cradled Mamá Sofía's head on my shoulders as she wept and wept. She and Papá Apolonio had married each other fifty-one years ago.

Mamá Sofía had been getting pains in her joints, and they seemed worse now. Herbal remedies brought her little relief. She said that this was because her mind had become diseased. Before the ambulance arrived, she had wrapped clean cloths around her knees covered with a paste made from the leaves she bought from a woman who sold herbs from door to door.

"Do you believe evil spirits live in the caves under the rivers, Luz Marina?" she asked me in all seriousness. "Our family has so many enemies now. Do you think someone is paying for harmful winds to blow only around our family?"

I remembered how Salvador used to consider me superstitious and how he used to laugh at what he called my "bush talk".

"I don't know, Mamá Sofía," I said, "but strange things happen in San Joaquín, that we know."

"Luz Marina, can't we fight it?"

"We can, Mamá Sofía. We are fighting it now."

"No, I mean can't we try to find a *H'men* who knows the prayers and medicines which will keep us safe?"

"Don't think like that, Mamá Sofía. We believe now in one God, we pray."

"When I was young, my parents always went to a *H'men* for help with curses and enchantments."

"We have been saved, Mamá Sofía," I said. "We are not cursed, we have been redeemed, as the pastor says."

"Perhaps we shouldn't talk any more about these things?" Mamá Sofía said.

I nodded. My mother made the sign of the cross, and I did the same.

The following morning, I left Mamá Sofía at the San Joaquín Hospital with Papá Apolonio and spent the entire day searching for a job in the shops around the Plaza San Joaquín. I entered a store that sold groceries.

I remembered that two or three years ago the owner had bought costumes from us for sale in his shop. His grown-up son was behind the cash register. He listened respectfully, using the time to polish his horn-rimmed glasses with a handkerchief he pulled from his back pocket.

"My father owns a club now, up on the hill." He pointed a chubby hand to the right. "I don't believe we need anyone. Business is slow." He glanced at the gold watch on his wrist. "But go ask him. He should be there at this time."

I wrote down the address he had given me, and made my way slowly up the hill towards a circular whitewashed building with a thatched roof. The sun made me giddy. I should have bought something to eat in the shop, but I had lost my appetite.

Inside the silent club, a waiter pointed across the small restaurant to where the owner, Señor Algarin, sat alone at a table eating his lunch. He was large and untidy. His shirt was draped over a chair and his paunch hung over his belt. Two empty beer bottles were on the table.

"Yes?" He didn't look up from his plate. His undershirt was smeared with tomato sauce. A lot of long black hair grew on his chest.

"Good afternoon. Do you have any vacancies?"

He glanced briefly at me, then looked at my face again. His eyes were close together under bushy eyebrows.

"What's your name?"

I told him, and he continued eating his *enchiladas*, nodding from time to time. "Have a seat. This is a bad time of the year. Maybe later I'll need some help."

"That's what your son said, but I thought I would take a chance anyway."

"What kind of job are you looking for?"

"Maybe I could work in the kitchen, something like that?"

He shook his head morosely. "I have a cook cranky as hell and you wouldn't last as many days as nights. His family works with him when we are busy."

I continued sitting at the table, reluctant to go back into the heat of the day to continue my search. The restaurant had an unobstructed view, on every side, of the surrounding countryside and the mountains in the distance.

"Thank you," I said, after some time, getting up from the table. I had decided not to remind him that he had once bought costumes from us. He was unlikely to remember a single vendor. Señor Algarin looked at me speculatively.

"There is one vacancy, but I am not sure you would want it."

"What kind is it?" I looked around the restaurant and bar, noticing a dance floor, a platform with a microphone and band instruments.

"You could do a little singing here. I'll bet you have a nice voice? What do you say?"

"I belong to Esperanza Evangelica, so I couldn't do that kind of work."

"It's an opportunity, lots of good tips. You would bring in new customers. A lot of people would pay good money to see what you look like."

He had recognised my name. Hanging my head in shame, I said goodbye. Walking downhill, I felt soiled, depressed, like a curiosity. Just imagine.

Mamá Sofía and I spent a second night sitting in the hospital corridor outside Papá Apolonio's ward. The doctors and nurses came and went. At about three o'clock in the morning my Papá Apolonio died. Mamá Sofía and I were there when his breath stopped. We telephoned Perla, and wrote a letter to Concha. Then we returned to sit in the hospital corridor.

Earlier, a nurse had removed the medical paraphernalia around Papá Apolonio's bed and pulled a sheet over his head. I had a blinding headache. Mamá Sofía cried and talked, talked and cried. At eight o'clock we walked to the post office. Mamá Sofía kissed the letter to Concha before dropping it into the box.

We were in the Elodio Alpuche Guerra rooms the first afternoon after my father's funeral, Mamá Sofía, Perla and I. Concha's telegram to Mamá Sofía lay on the table. "Poor Concha," Mamá Sofía had said. "She wanted to be here, I know."

The rooms looked bare, and the floor was littered with scraps of paper, cloth and bits of sewing thread. We had spent the day packing. It was still raining off and on, and we were silent as we worked.

Papá Apolonio's funeral had been short and simple. He was buried in the San Joaquín Cemetery near to the graves of Mamá Sofía's parents. There were not too many people at the funeral, but I noticed Salvador's brother, Andrés, standing with his driver a few yards away.

It surprised me a little to see Andrés there, but not too much. Like his father, Don Pablo, Andrés considered himself a grand *patrón*. He took great pride in this role, which sometimes caused him to do unpredictable things. I didn't know if my mother and sister had seen him, and I had not mentioned his presence.

Mamá Sofía and Perla wept all through the funeral and into the night. Seeing the breath leave Papá Apolonio's body had the opposite effect on me. I have not cried, because something inside me does not really believe he has died. As long as I have memory, Papá Apolonio lives. I won't tell the doctor these thoughts about my father. This is the kind of thing that makes her tap her pen on the notepad. "Interesting," she might say.

Eventually, the night of Papá Apolonio's funeral, we went to bed but I doubt if anyone got very much sleep and we were up before sunrise the following day. I looked out at the twinkling lights of San Joaquín on the distant hillsides with a feeling of dread.

Mamá Sofía was not saying very much because she was hoping that Perla would be able to offer us a place in her home. She lived with her husband and two children in a nice home in Corozal, many miles away from San Joaquín. The house had a downstairs apartment which was rented out. I did not want to leave San Joaquín, but I wondered if Perla would be able to have Mamá in her home.

Perla's husband, Javier Barrios Delgado, was a tall, thin, snobbish man, who concentrated on cultivating the right people. He had risen in his profession through hard work and scholarships. His actions seemed to indicate that he wanted very little to do with his less successful relatives, let alone a notorious one like myself.

I looked over at Perla who now sat at the table, dressed in black slacks and a white shirt. She was talking about poor Papá Apolonio as she looked at Mamá Sofía and myself sweeping the floor and tidying the room in preparation for our departure.

Perla began to snap and unsnap the large gilt clasp of her leather handbag. She opened a black powder compact, peered at her long, narrow face in the mirror, applying fresh lipstick to her tiny mouth. She glanced at the large face of a watch which covered most of her slender wrist.

Earlier Perla had helped us to pack the boxes of food and clothing, including Papá Apolonio's, which was hard for all of us. We couldn't bear to part with the worn-out shirts, trousers and sandals just yet, but agreed that later on we might give them away.

"Mamá Sofía, Luz Marina," Perla said, getting up from her chair. "When are you going to stop that sweeping and get dressed? The pastor will soon be here."

We were surprised. Mamá Sofía, her white hair loose on her shoulders, her tiny feet encased in an old pair of my father's shoes, looked at me, and then at Perla.

"Ay," Mamá Sofía said. "Why didn't you tell me before? Did you know, Luz Marina?"

I shook my head, but suspected that, as is her way, Perla had been up to some sort of scheming behind Mamá Sofía's back. I am not sure, but I think that Perla is Mamá Sofía's favourite daughter.

Before that most terrible night of my life, Mamá Sofía marvelled continuously about Perla's wedding, her successful husband and her intelligent children. I don't know for certain what her husband does. I think it is something Perla refers to as "on the way up" in the public service because they are not rich.

"Oh," Perla was saying to Mamá Sofía. "I forgot about it until just a while ago. I was talking to the pastor at Papá's funeral and he mentioned that he would visit us this afternoon. I am not sure why. Perhaps he can help us decide what to do."

Shortly after three that afternoon, the pastor drove his van through a field, where cattle grazed. He negotiated the muddy path to our rooms with great adroitness, using the randomly placed concrete slabs which led to the door of our rooms.

The afternoon was still humid, but he appeared fresh and unharried. He carried a Bible in one hand, jingling the keys in his pocket with the other. I remembered the days when he used to walk, or ride an old bicycle, from door to door.

I always felt deeply embarrassed in the pastor's presence, although he had never, so much as by a word or by a look, referred to the money Salvador took from the church to pay his gambling debts. Pastor Felipe Rivas Ortega had cared deeply, perhaps still did, for Salvador Joaquín, who returned his affection for as long as his illness allowed him to care about anyone outside of himself.

"Afternoon, afternoon," the pastor said, wiping his shoes on the rubber mat outside the door. "My condolences once again." He bowed his head politely to us, a half smile hovering around his mouth. The pastor sang like an angel and preached the word of God in a strong, beautiful voice filled with emotion.

I still held the broom in my hand. As I leaned it against a wall, I noticed the pile of dirt near the doorway, several dead cockroaches and a lizard, shrivelled to a black stringiness. Ay, *Dios*.

"Good afternoon, Pastor," Perla said. "Thank you. Thank you. Please come in and have a seat."

The pastor sat on the edge of a chair around the unvarnished table. He said many pleasant things about Papá Apolonio, who had been one of Esperanza Evangelica's best fundraisers. He glanced at the cardboard boxes piled in one corner and at Mamá Sofía, whose cheeks were wet with tears.

"Señora," he said, addressing Mamá Sofía, "and Luz Marina." He turned to where I stood in the doorway. "Perla and I spoke briefly after the funeral yesterday. She told me about your situation. I was sorry to hear about it. But these things happen."

"People say God never gives us more than we can bear," Mamá Sofía said.

"Indeed, Señora, which is why I am here."

Mamá Sofía's lips were trembling as she looked at Perla. "I am glad," Mamá Sofía said, "that God has given me children who can help me in my old age."

"Yes, indeed," the pastor replied. "Perla explained to me how sad she feels that it is not possible for you and Luz Marina to live with her."

"Perla," I said, "let Mamá live with you. I can find another job here. I want to stay near my children."

Perla began to cry. She hugged Mamá Sofía, and the two of them were crying together. "I can't take you in, Mamá, I wish I could. But Luz Marina will be with you." Both Mamá Sofía and I understood that Perla's husband would not welcome either of us in his home. Still, Mamá Sofía had been hoping for a change in his heart.

"Don't worry, Mamá," I said. "Remember how we've talked about opening a little stall in Plaza San Joaquín? We've saved a little. We'll manage, Mamá Sofía."

"But is it enough," Mamá Sofía said, "for food and rent, and the licence and I don't know what?" I felt she had almost completely lost her faith and her trust in me.

"A stall in the plaza?" Perla said. "Are you out of your mind?

Mamá doesn't have the strength to do that kind of work any more. What can I do, Mamá Sofía, what can I do?"

"You are doing all you can, Perla. If things were different in your family, you'd take us in, I know."

The pastor cleared his throat, looking down at the dirt floor, as though he was frightened of the words he had to say. "I have had a most generous offer from Andrés Casal." He tried to smile at our shocked and troubled faces.

"Andrés Casal? Salvador's brother?" Perla asked. Even she was dumbfounded.

"Yes," the pastor said. "After the funeral, he asked me to convey his condolences to you. He also wants you to know how sorry he is for his mother's actions."

"Sorry?" I said, incredulous, wondering what had happened in the Casal family to cause him to send his regrets for Doña Catalina's actions. I suspected a trick, but Perla was urging the pastor to go on. In the past our connection with the Casal family was something Perla's husband had valued.

"As you know, Andrés runs the Caana Hotel in the mountains. He employs many people."

"Yes," Perla replied. "My husband attended a conference there once. I went with him. The dining room is on posts, so high up it feels as if you are truly in a palace in the sky."

"When was that?" Mamá Sofía asked.

"Oh, I can't remember, Mamá," Perla said. "It was a long time before Luz's trial, that I know." She stopped abruptly. Mamá Sofía's face looked stern and cold. I thought she had become angry at the mention of my trial, but she said, "But you didn't come to see us then, Perla. Why? Papá Apolonio so looked forward to your visits. So do I."

"I wanted to stop by, Mamá Sofía. I thought we would have time on the last day, but we needed to drive straight back. I am sorry."

"In any case," the pastor said, "Andrés Casal is offering you a job in his hotel, and room in the staff quarters. It is a magnificent offer, made in all humility Andrés told me in reparation for his sins in the past."

"No," I said, shocked. "I can't accept."

"Who are you to talk about accepting or not accepting, Luz Marina?" Perla was enraged. "What do you think you are going to do? Walk the streets for the rest of your life?"

"No!" I said. "I am going to work. There must be all kinds of work."

"Who else will hire you around here? Here is Andrés offering you a job he could fill ten times over, and a place to live and you are refusing to think about it. You should be thanking your lucky stars, crawling on your hands and knees after, after ..."

"After I killed his brother Salvador Joaquín? What do you know about it, Perla? Were you there that night? Did you ever ask me what happened?"

"Shut up, Perla," Mamá Sofía shouted. "I said to shut up both of you." Mamá Sofía slumped forward in her chair. She gasped for air.

"That's you all over, Luz Marina," Perla said, "nothing but trouble, from ever since!"

The pastor looked very embarrassed. He mopped his face with his handkerchief, and tried his best to say the right things.

We carried my mother to the bed my father had used. Perla fanned Mamá Sofía's face vigorously with a straw fan. In small sips, Mamá Sofía drank the water I held to her mouth. After a few minutes, I held Mamá Sofía's head and looked into her eyes. "Shall we go to Andrés's palace in the sky, Mamá?"

At first she looked uncertain. She shook her head, her fingers playing with the folds of her faded black skirt. "No. We shouldn't go to Caana."

"Why not?" Perla was asking. "For the love of God, why not? The court said you are not guilty, Luz Marina, and Andrés clearly agrees. Give it a try." She hugged my shoulders. "It might be your salvation, Luz Marina – our salvation."

I turned to the pastor. "Give me some time to think about it, please."

"I understand that it is very unexpected. I myself was surprised. But I reminded myself that God works in mysterious ways. Perhaps Andrés remembers, as I do, how much Salvador loved you."

"And I loved him," I said to the pastor.

"I am very well aware of that," the pastor said. He looked around, "Let me help you move away from here. Where did you plan to live?"

"I've booked a room at a small boarding house on a side street off Plaza San Joaquín. It's above Nora's Restaurant."

"I know the place," the pastor said. "Very fair rates. Shall we close up here and go?"

At Nora's Restaurant and boarding house, Perla and the pastor helped us to carry the boxes up the stairs into the room. After he had left, Mamá Sofía and I walked with Perla to the bus station. In spite of everything, she looked well groomed with her short haircut, her high cheekbones slightly rouged, and her clothes unwrinkled. Perla's hooked nose reminded me of Papá Apolonio's.

She hugged me briefly and I was glad to be released because, for some reason, I don't like to be touched very much any more. The doctor told me that I now connect caresses with pain, but that I would get over it, in time. Perhaps she is right.

Perla pressed something into my hand, closing my fingers over a tiny ball of tissue paper. "They're worth something. I'll tell Javier that I lost them."

I looked at her again and saw that her earlobes were empty. In the paper were the golden filigree earrings her husband had given her as a wedding gift and which he liked her to wear regularly.

"I wouldn't know where to sell these, Perla. I am afraid of going back to prison."

"Don't be so silly, Luz Marina."

"I understand the sacrifice, Perlita," I said, kissing her briefly on the cheek, placing the earrings in the pocket of her blouse. "See you soon?"

"Very soon, Luz Marinita, very soon."

Mamá Sofía had tears in her eyes, glad, I feel sure, that we were no longer quarrelling. We didn't fight very much as girls, Perla, Concha and I. We considered ourselves a team against all opponents. I know that I have let down my sisters who have worked so hard to better themselves in this life.

As Perla was about to board the bus for Belize City, she tried to press a knotted handkerchief into Mamá Sofía's hand, but she wouldn't take the money. Perla, looking very sombre, didn't try again. She slipped the earrings and money into her bag and snapped it shut. "I'll be back as soon as I can, Mamá Sofía," she said.

"I know, Perla, I know. Take care of yourself and my grandchildren." We waved until the bus rolled across the Caracol Bridge.

Mamá Sofía and I walked back towards the plaza, not saying very much to each other. I felt my spirits lifting a little. Perhaps it was the thought that Feliciano, Teresa and Eduardo were only a few yards away. I would soon see them, I was sure. Would they recognise me? As soon as I returned to the room, I would try to do something about my appearance.

I expected Mamá Sofía to cry and be depressed after Perla had gone. Instead she said, "Before we go back to the room, let's walk around a little, Luz Marina. Perhaps we can find out how much it costs to rent a stall in the plaza."

We walked up and down until late into the night, trying not to remember that Papá Apolonio was no longer with us.

Part 3

It proved to be far more expensive for us to rent a stall than we had expected. The vendors who paid the town board for space in the plaza told us they were unable to rent a portion of a stall on a weekly basis. We decided to visit the town board office ourselves the following day. Perhaps we would be able to get a licence. During that night my mother began complaining of feeling a little feverish. The next day, however, she seemed to recover her energy.

After breakfast, we walked to the town board, not far from the police station, to submit our application. The waiting list was very long and there was no telling how long it would take before we might obtain space in the plaza.

"It's because we don't have any political connections," Mamá Sofía said. "That's how things work in San Joaquín."

"I know, Mamá Sofía," I replied. "It is something to think about. How can we get connected to them?"

"Only the good *Dios* knows," Mamá Sofía said. "Usually we would need to do something for them, maybe?"

"I don't think there's anything we can do," I said, trying not to think of the meeting in Elodio Alpuche Guerra's office. It is hard to believe that I can no longer return there. My old life seems to be continually at war with this new one, and often I feel very disoriented.

"Let's wait and see," Mamá Sofía said. "You never know. Life is large, as your Papá Apolonio used to tell us."

On our way back to the boarding house, we were caught in a downpour. By the time we reached the room, Mamá Sofía's fever had returned. She took some aspirins and tried to rest. But as the night wore on, she became worse. I placed cold compresses on her forehead for most of the night, fearful that she might become delirious.

Before daylight, I telephoned a doctor recommended by the owner of Nora's Restaurant. After the doctor had examined Mamá Sofía, he said she should rest in bed for a few days. After he left, I filled the prescription at a nearby pharmacy. There were four windows in our room, and I kept the slats of the green jalousies tilted against the light which hurt Mamá Sofía's eyes. I was grateful that the room was cool, even during the daytime.

All day, and for most of the night, the sounds of car horns, bicycle bells and voices were loud in our room. During those days, my mother sometimes spoke of the days when my sisters and I were in primary school, my father worked on the *milpa*, and she took care of our house and garden. Perhaps because we were now in a room very close to the plaza, she often thought of Papá Apolonio's fight with his friend during that festival night long ago.

At other times she spoke bitterly of Doña Catalina and her family, cursing her own simpleness, and Papá Apolonio's, for believing that Salvador would ever marry me. These were difficult days for us, as I tried to restore her strength with soups from the downstairs restaurant, which she didn't care for very much. However, she ate most of the fruit I purchased in the plaza.

One afternoon, for the first time, she asked me about prison and the trial. I noticed, however, that it made her extremely agitated to listen, so I kept my replies short. She liked me to repeat the words of the judge who had said, "I have considered your case very carefully, and I don't intend to keep you in prison for one minute more."

"Quite right, too, quite right," she murmured sometimes as she fell asleep. I tried to make light of the misery and terror of those days which are beginning to seem unreal. But sometimes I dream of my prison cell, and I am always so relieved to wake up and find I am not there.

By the following Sunday, Mamá Sofía was well enough to go out, so we went to sit together on a bench in the plaza underneath the umbrella-shaped trees. We were not far from Doña Catalina's house, and the Church of San Joaquín. My mother said she wanted to go to mass again so we made our way slowly to the church, pausing by the huge stone angels on either side of the door. The branches of several royal palm trees brushed the rooftop of the church. The bells in the towers were ringing out across the town.

"It's the same God as Evangelica's, no?" Mamá Sofía said, as we entered.

"I believe it is," I replied. "The pastor will understand, I feel sure."

We paused for a moment, inhaling the incense and the scent of burning candles. We stared at the Chapel of Our Lady of Sorrows where I last sat with my children. Mamá Sofía pointed to the statue on the altar. "She answered our prayers, Luz Marina."

In the chapel we lit candles we had bought, one for Papá Apolonio and one for Salvador Joaquín. I prayed for help to accept my situation to which I find it difficult to become reconciled, and for the safe return to us of Feliciano, Teresa and Eduardo.

Early for the eleven o'clock mass, we sat near a window, staring out at the side wall and windows of Doña Catalina's house which overlooked the gardens of the Church of San Joaquín. Sitting there listening to the church bells, it was hard not to remember that Sunday long ago, when Doña Catalina began to suspect that Don Pablo had left for good.

She had searched the house, rifling through papers, looking for a note, but there had not been any. Later on, Doña Catalina, outwardly calm, strolled with me around the gardens and the orchards, fragrant with orange blossoms. But the servants and workers shook their heads. They had no information about Don Pablo. Returning to the house, we sat on the *galeria* until it was time for mass.

"Things cannot go on in this way, Luz Marina," Doña Catalina said. "Of course, he has never cared for this house as I do. He wanted to continue living the *hacienda* life on our first estate except that he was seldom there."

Doña Catalina enjoyed the house on Avenue Cahal Pech because at any time of the day or night she could step downstairs into the street, where she was well known, and mingle with the crowds, absorbing energy, feeling youthful for a while. "I am not a country person," she often said, "I like to see life about me."

As we left the house that evening for five o'clock mass, I said, "It's a little strange that Don Pablo has not sent word, Doña Catalina."

"It is, Luz Marina," she said, lifting the white mantilla off her shoulders and arranging it carefully on her hair. The bells were still ringing as we walked the short distance to the church on Avenue Cahal Pech.

After mass was over, she approached Padre Alfredo Aldana, who had married her and Don Pablo. Although Don Pablo seldom attended mass, the priest was her husband's chief confidant in the village. If Don Pablo had left any message, it would surely be with Padre Alfredo. The priest told her that, as she had already suspected, he had gone, perhaps for good.

"I delayed telling you, Catalina, because I hoped he would change his mind."

"But can you tell me why, Padre?" Doña Catalina asked, bowing her head so that he would not observe the passionate anger, the bewilderment, in her eyes.

The padre shrugged, "Pablo did not really say why, although I tried to press him. He asked me to tell you that it was necessary for him to leave. I was a witness to his will. The house, what's left of the estate, all that's there belongs to you and your sons."

"Where do you think he has gone, Padre?"

The priest was silent for a while, looking over Doña Catalina's bowed head, nodding to parishioners, allowing his eyes to linger on the church, its cream-coloured walls and open windows. "I can't honestly tell you, Catalina. I have no idea. Perhaps he returned to Mexico. He had a fondness for Spanish ways, maybe he went to Madrid or Barcelona, places he wanted to visit, continuing his journey, so to speak."

The priest fell silent, adjusting the broad black leather belt he wore around his cassock. He folded his arms across his chest. "Pablo was not a bad man, Catalina, we all know that. He was always extremely generous to the church. We will miss his support. And it seemed to me that he had been a good husband and father, these past years?"

Doña Catalina nodded.

"But you know, Catalina, I have asked myself, often, why he stayed in San Joaquín. Now I ask myself, why did he leave? People do strange things. Perhaps you should search your heart, Catalina, perhaps the answer is there?"

Doña Catalina drew her mantilla more closely about her head and shoulders. "Thank you, Padre," she replied. "I will do as you suggest." She took my arm and we began walking away. She did not turn around when the priest called, "You are always welcome to visit me here. I shall miss the talks we used to have, you, Pablo and I."

"Thank you, Padre, I shall remember that," Doña Catalina replied. But she did not extend an invitation to the padre for Sunday dinner as Don Pablo used to do. The priest would probably miss the evenings on the patio with Don Pablo when they had enjoyed

Rufina's fine cooking, and the wines Don Pablo chose with such care from the cellar he had constructed below the house.

As the candles were being lit by the altar boys, I turned my face away from Doña Catalina's house and faced the altar. Mamá Sofía's head was bowed over her black beads. I ached with pity, looking at the roughness of her fingers, the protruding knuckles of her arthritic hands. I too bowed my head.

Kneeling there, I thought of the boarding house which was proving to be more costly than we had imagined. We ate frugally, mostly fruit and vegetables from the market. At night we sat at one of the tables at a plaza stall and ordered whatever was cheapest, usually beans with tortillas or beans with rice. Afterwards we sat together in our darkened room at a window overlooking the plaza.

We talked until late, or sat silently staring at the activity in the plaza, or at the shops, stores and other fine houses like Doña Catalina's which ranged along the four sides. If I did not find employment soon, we could find ourselves sleeping on a bench in the plaza with only our few belongings to cushion our heads.

Most of the really nice things, like the furniture, Papá Apolonio's tools, my books and Mamá Sofía's colourful hammocks, had been sold. When I left Salvador's house for the last time, I took nothing with me. All we had left now were two suitcases with clothes, a few family pictures, the sewing machine and official papers like birth and marriage certificates.

A few minutes after the mass began, my mother placed a hand on my arm and squeezed it gently. I looked in the direction of her eyes and saw Andrés Casal enter a pew on the far side of the church with a few people I did not recognise.

I knew what Mamá Sofía was thinking. She looked imploringly at me. I nodded slightly, and she brought my hand to her mouth and I kissed it. I cried silently, feeling as though I had lost an important battle. Mamá Sofía kept squeezing my hand tightly in hers. During the mass, I listened to my poor Mamá Sofía's quavering responses to the priest at the altar. The fear of poverty had led us towards a pact that seemed to me to be beyond shame.

The next day, Monday, Mamá Sofía was feeling a little off colour again. After she had eaten a breakfast of tea, bread and bananas, I left her propped up in the bed we shared. Her thick grey hair was spread out on the pillow. A glass of water and a bottle of prescription tablets were on the table beside her. I wanted to catch an early bus to Andrés's Caana Hotel, situated about six miles from the Plaza San Joaquín.

I was very nervous. I dressed as neatly as I could in my dark clothes, flat shoes and my big bag which went with me everywhere. It didn't have very much in it: my purse, a red lipstick, a powder compact, a comb, and pictures of my children in an envelope. Sometimes I looked at the pictures to remind myself that life might be better some day.

But as the weeks went by, I did this less often. Perhaps I was growing discouraged. I didn't feel very hopeful about this trip. I thought of telephoning the hotel for an appointment. But I knew if I was given an appointment for tomorrow or the following week I would never keep it.

The rain was holding off and after the bus had travelled higher into the hills, the sun began to shine. It was quite hot by the time the bus reached the turn-off for Andrés's hotel. I tried not to think too much about the coming meeting. If Andrés did give me a job, I quite understood that I would, in all probability, be re-entering an old nightmare. But as my Papá Apolonio once told me, sometimes the quickest way to dry road was through the mud.

Andrés's hotel was different from most of the hotels in the area around San Joaquín. The rooms for guests were built to resemble the exteriors of village huts. Maids wearing white blouses and black skirts walked to and fro, carrying piles of towels, sheets, buckets, brooms and mops. Through the doorways, I saw gleaming bathrooms and colourful bedspreads.

In the lobby I gave my name to the young man, who was hanging keys on a board of hooks. I told him I had come to enquire about a job. "There are no vacancies, Señora," he said.

"Señor Casal said I should come here and apply."

"Today?"

"He didn't say any special time."

The clerk, adjusting the bowtie on his white shirt, spoke quietly into a telephone on the mahogany counter. As he listened, his dark eyes looked out across the expanse of hills, from which the clouds were slowly lifting. Replacing the receiver, he said, "Someone will soon come to take you to the office."

I sat on one of the cane chairs so like the ones on the *galeria* of Doña Catalina's house. The cushions were covered with a bright floral cloth. Giant ferns grew outside the door of the lobby. The red tiles looked cool and clean. I looked down at my feet encased in blue plastic shoes. They weren't too bad, except after a long walk in the hot sun; then my feet burned as if they were on fire.

Eventually, another young man arrived and asked me to follow him. We walked along paths through the grounds. I inhaled the scent of freshly mown grass and the flowering bushes and trees. It was absolutely quiet except for occasional birdcalls. Each cottage we passed had a covered, screened patio. On some of them, foreign and local guests were seated at tables having lunch. Others were inside the main restaurant, built up high and shaded by ancient trees, which Perla had mentioned.

I wiped my clammy palms on my skirt. The young man did not say anything to me as we walked, although he was as gently courteous as the first. He held open the door so that I could enter. There were about twelve people in the large room, busy at desks, talking into telephones, or moving back and forth between adjoining offices.

In a little while the young man returned to lead me into Andrés's office. It was quite small. His desk was set between two windows. There were beautiful paintings of animals and birds on the wall. From the doorway, I gazed at Andrés's sombre face, into his wide, round innocent-looking brown eyes fringed with long eyelashes. He had the smooth skin of a young boy. I knew that he was only about an inch taller than myself. His thinning hair reminded me of his father, Don Pablo.

"Good morning, Señor." As usual, he wore a white silk shirt with ballooning sleeves, a thin gold chain around his neck, and a thick, heavy *esclava* of gleaming gold around his hairy wrist. I didn't need to see his trousers to know that they would be of fine material, dark and baggy, in the latest fashion. His shoes, I was sure, were of shining black patent leather.

"My condolences, Miss Figueroa," Andrés said, not getting up. He leaned back in his chair, but I knew he was as nervous as I was. "Let's not be formal with each other." He opened his eyes very wide.

"Thank you for attending Papá Apolonio's funeral."

"I wanted to pay my last respects," Andrés said. "We talked together once or twice."

"With Papá Apolonio?" I asked.

"Yes. Your father was a nice man. Please, Luz Marina, sit down."

I walked across the beige carpet to the chair beside his desk. "The pastor at Esperanza Evangelica said you might have work that I could do?"

"Well," he said, lighting a cigar and shaking the spent match several times before dropping it into an ashtray, "I remember

114

that you spent a lot of time working in the garden of our home." He smiled.

"Yes." I gazed up at a painting of a jaguar peering through a tangle of bushes, and I thought of Doña Catalina.

"It's an outdoor job, working with the gardener in charge of providing the kitchen with fresh vegetables. The pay is small, but we provide room and board."

"I am responsible for my mother," I replied, wondering if Doña Catalina ever brought my children to Andrés's hotel. "She is welcome to stay with you, of course."

"When can we begin?" I thought of Andrés's unceasing rivalry with Salvador, and the fact that a gardener's job would keep me far away from his office.

He was looking at me with the greatest curiosity, and did not reply to my question. "I was sorry to hear from my mother that things did not work out for you at Elodio Alpuche Guerra's *rancho*."

"They didn't," I replied.

"He can be stubborn in certain areas, but then so can my mother." We sat silently for a moment or two, as he glanced through the window to the right of his desk. The grounds of the Caana Hotel stretched to the Río Caracol, a long way from where we sat. "We would need you to start as soon as possible."

"I will try to get here on Wednesday."

"Good," Andrés said. "Inform the young man who brought you in. A hotel van will collect you with the other employees from San Joaquín. The times are posted on the bulletin board near the outside door."

"Thank you."

"You're quite welcome. As I told the pastor, I am anxious to help the congregation at Esperanza Evangelica. Salvador made it almost a tradition in our family, no? As I remember, my family is indebted to the pastor there."

I hung my head, remembering that I had once asked Andrés about the dory of flower petals. In desperation, I had spoken with him on the telephone when Salvador began gambling heavily. I had called him again about the large sum of money Salvador had embezzled from Esperanza Evangelica. Salvador had accused me of disloyalty.

Andrés walked to the door and opened it. As I was going through, he said, "And how are you feeling these days?" I knew he was referring to my release from prison.

"Very much better. Thank you, Andrés."

"At your service," he replied.

I was in the corridor before I quite believed that I had a job, and shelter for my mother and myself. I closed the door and stood quietly for a moment before returning to the main office. As I walked along the carpeted floor I found myself repeating, like Don Pablo's parrots, "Too, too incredible."

Thinking of Don Pablo's parrots reminded me of the morning following Doña Catalina's visit to Padre Alfredo at the Church of San Joaquín. The rain was clattering on the roof when I entered Doña Catalina's room. She stood at a window staring down at the plaza. She had not slept, and accepted the coffee I placed in her hands with a nod of gratitude.

After she had finished dressing, I followed her to her husband's rooms at the top of the house. As we climbed the curving stairs, she said, "Did I ever tell you how Don Pablo came to be in Belize, Luz Marina?"

"No, Señora."

"He was on a sailing holiday with some friends. The boat needed repairs so they stayed longer than they'd expected. Don Pablo used the time to travel to San Joaquín and other places."

"Yes, Señora?"

"Yes. The opportunity to buy cheap land excited him. By then his friends were quarrelling among themselves. Eventually they abandoned the boat and went their separate ways."

"*Ay, Dios*, Señora."

"Indeed, Luz Marina."

Doña Catalina wandered through the rooms, hesitantly at first, but then more confidently. They were still filled with the smell of tobacco. Don Pablo's leather sandals were beneath his bed, his pens strewn across the desk.

Pulling open the huge mirrored doors of the wardrobe, she rummaged around until she discovered a bunch of keys on a long silver chain. Most of Don Pablo's clothing had been left behind, except for a few good suits, his overcoat, his expensive watch from Switzerland, a photograph of his parents, things he took with him whenever he travelled outside Belize. Doña Catalina crossed to his desk. She unlocked the drawers and opened a chequebook.

"Well, Luz Marina," she said. "He's comfortable wherever he is." She ran an index finger along the frame of a map of the world above his desk.

Doña Catalina felt sure that her husband was travelling around the world, continuing to do what he had been doing when they first met. His life in San Joaquín had been an interruption of his ambition to see all the strange places and people he had ever read about. She also knew, she said, that he would never return, that he would continue travelling for as long as his money lasted, which would be for a considerable length of time.

"It's amazing to me, Luz Marina, that I did not understand this before, when it was all perfectly clear."

She continued to talk, not expecting me to reply, as she pulled out drawer after drawer of the enormous desk. The drawers were almost completely empty, except for the account books for the

117

estate. She sat down at the desk and picked up the telephone. He had trained her well. The business of the day must be dealt with before personal matters like grief.

On her return from mass the evening before she had summoned her sons, and told them about their father's departure. They had eaten together outdoors on the patio off the main dining room, looking towards the hills.

Doña Catalina sat at Don Pablo's desk for most of the day, eating little, taking small sips of cold water from a glass I refilled every now and then. She spoke out loud sometimes as though to herself, or to give me instructions for Rufina.

She continued poring over the figures, staring as if for the first time at the strong, flamboyant character of Don Pablo's script, the little flourishes at the end of certain words, the enormous capital letters.

Don Pablo had been an educated man. He received books, papers and letters from all over the world. From him, Doña Catalina said, she had received the greater part of any education she had.

After Luis was born, Don Pablo had set up his own rooms at the top of the house. At the end of that long day, I followed Doña Catalina as she wandered around the large rooms he had designed. The shelves were lined with books, papers and files. Now and then she would say to me, "See, that's gone," or "He's taken the clay figurines."

There were large windows in every wall with views of the citrus orchards and the blue hills in the distance. Don Pablo had enjoyed riding around the land on his horse, or in one of the trucks. Standing at a window beside Doña Catalina, I heard, in my mind, Don Pablo's voice saying, "Coldness? Indifference?" or "That is a fantasy, Catalina," or "Can't you see that I am reading?" or "Don't interrupt me when I'm working, please."

I thought of mealtimes, day after day, when she and I ate alone on the *galeria* or in the dining room when it rained, listening to the sounds from the garden and the ticking of the huge clock which Don Pablo had imported from overseas.

Doña Catalina did not care for the clock. She said its face was too large. It ticked too loudly in the silence. The huge pendulum swinging backwards and forwards made her dizzy, if she happened to stare at it for any length of time.

Doña Catalina touched the sparkling glass decanter, half-filled with the dry sherry Don Pablo enjoyed. She brought a used glass to her nose, and then replaced the glass carefully on the silver tray. She poured herself some of the sherry, using a clean glass. She leaned against the arms of a leather chair facing the window. "Once," Doña Catalina said, "I asked him about these rooms. He said he had furnished them from memory."

After that day, Doña Catalina became quite a different person. She and I no longer sat together on the *galeria*. She gave away the parrots to Rufina's relatives, sent Don Pablo's dogs away to be sold, and hired several more guards. Every morning, Doña Catalina left for the estate offices before nine o'clock.

In the evenings she sat in Don Pablo's rooms and read the books and papers he had left behind. If she was quiet in those rooms, it was from choice, not because she had been silenced, as before, by a look, a word, or a gesture; not because she had been dismissed by the flick of a light switch.

In the gardens of the Caana Hotel, I pressed one foot hard on the shovel, pushing it into the soil, fighting back tears of anger as I listened to Mamá Sofía murmuring to Hector, the old gardener to whom we had been assigned.

"I don't mind, Señora Sofía," Hector was saying, "if you take a few green peppers and tomatoes. Divide the bruised ones into two piles, one for you and one for me."

"Thank you, Señor," Mamá Sofía said. The gardener lifted his hat to my mother before continuing to roll his wheelbarrow of vegetables to the hotel kitchen.

"Luz Marina, tonight we'll make the sauce, all right?"

"Yes, Mamá Sofía," I said. For a while we worked silently, listening to the rattle of pots and pans and the voices from the kitchen overlooking the vegetable garden. Rows and rows of vegetable plants and fruit trees surrounded us.

Mamá Sofía and I wore long-sleeved shirts and trousers to prevent the bugs from biting us. At least there were no mosquitoes buzzing around our ears this morning. I was still learning to be grateful for small mercies and to take comfort in simple pleasures.

A few yards away, hotel guests sat in the lower dining room, and on the patios, eating breakfast or drinking coffee. Talk and laughter reached us through the barrier of trees. Birds were chattering wildly. The early morning drizzle and the overcast sky had given way to hazy sunlight shimmering on the bright green leaves of the tall trees.

The coolness of early morning had gone. I was sweating and my stomach heaved at the acidic stench of the manure that I was mixing into the soil. My knee-high rubber boots were covered with mud. Hair straggled about my face, and I paused, leaning sideways to re-do the length of my plait which had unravelled.

I looked up at the elevated dining room encircled almost entirely by the top branches of shade trees. Salvador had been the first person to tell me that the word *caana* probably means sky palace. Don Pablo had named the hotel after a temple at the ruins of Caracol.

I thought, too, of the Sunday afternoon, perhaps a year after Don Pablo had left, when Salvador pulled me along the broad corridor of the house on Avenue Cahal Pech to Doña Catalina's bedroom. Outside the door, I said to him softly, "Not in this way, Salva. Let's wait until Doña Catalina is alone, please?"

"No, Luz Marina, now." His face above mine was red and blotchy. I had rarely seen him so upset; it scared and puzzled me.

"See!" Salvador said, fanning my face furiously with the white envelope. It contained a single proof of the wedding invitation which he was planning to have printed. I had not known he was going to do this. He wanted to surprise me, so he said.

After lunch that day, the dining room doors remained closed. The voices of Doña Catalina, Salvador, Andrés and Luis became louder and louder. It was mid-afternoon before Rufina and I were able to clear the dishes and cloth from the table.

The dining room seemed in unusual disarray with wine glasses on the floor and on the window ledges. The chairs were out of their usual places, and I found a table napkin on the sideboard with the huge mirror in a gilded frame. I wondered what important event had happened there. Andrés and Luis had followed Doña Catalina to her room.

"Well?" Salvador said to me now. "Shall we go in?"

"You go in first, Salvador, I feel too shy. Truly."

He gave me one of his sidelong glances, calling out, "Madre?" as he turned the brass knob on the door of Doña Catalina's bedroom. "Luz Marina and I have something to show you." He placed the invitation on the table beside his mother's bed. "We wanted you to be the first to know."

I did not follow Salvador into the room. My knees felt wobbly and my heart was beating much too quickly; I was both happy and scared. I hoped Doña Catalina would be understanding. I believed, then, that she knew me very well, that she cared for me, even loved me.

Andrés was staring through a window, perhaps at the statue of the goddess Don Pablo had erected on the patio all those years ago. His face looked glum, his thoughts seemed very far away.

Luis, the quietest of Doña Catalina's sons, sat on a love-seat between her dressing table and the huge bed. He stroked his drooping moustache before picking up the envelope and handing it to his mother.

She had been lying, fully dressed, against the bolsters on her bed, but now she sat up, swinging her legs over the side. Luis picked up the small black pumps from the floor and slipped them on her stockinged feet. There were dark circles under her eyes, and her lipstick was slightly smudged. She had grown thinner, and her rings were loose on her fingers.

After reading the invitation, her eyes flew to Salvador's face, "You are being thoughtless, unkind to your family," she said, returning the card and envelope to Luis. She did not glance at the doorway, and I immediately felt chilled to the bone.

Luis, who nearly always wore three-piece grey suits that seemed far too big for him, picked up his glasses from the table. He looked briefly at the card in his hand. Removing his glasses, he bit the handles and said to Salvador, "This is an embarrassment to us." He passed the card to Andrés who read it, before dropping it on the chair beside him.

"Uncalled for and unnecessary," Andrés said.

"I think it is exactly the other way around," Salvador said. Even to me, his voice sounded too harsh. "What is 'embarrassing' about wanting to marry Luz Marina?"

"You are deliberately misunderstanding Luis, as usual, Salvador," Doña Catalina said.

"Luz Marina!" Salvador called, turning around to see where I was.

Luis placed a restraining hand on his arm. "Just a minute, Salvador." He crossed the room swiftly. He had a gentle voice. "Excuse us, Luz Marina, please," he said to me. "Wait for Salvador in your room, or anywhere you like." He closed the door.

It was nearly night before Salvador came to find me. I was sitting at the servants' table outside the kitchen. Stars were already twinkling in the sky, a darkening blue. To my relief, Salvador seemed a lot calmer. I looked at his face eagerly, hoping that Doña Catalina had asked to talk with me. He sat on the bench beside me, brushing my hair away from my face, linking his fingers with mine.

"You are to pack up your things tonight, Luz Marina. Tomorrow morning I will drive you home." I thought of my Papá Apolonio and my Mamá Sofía who would be glad that Salvador and I had decided on a date to be married. Perla and Concha were going to be bridesmaids. They would be so excited.

"Is Doña Catalina angry with me, Salvador? Won't she see me?"

He shook his head. "She is angry with me more than you. But she and I have been quarrelling over various matters for a long time. Forget about it, Luz Marina. Tomorrow we'll both get away from this place of ticks."

I looked at him questioningly, wondering how he could make jokes at such a time. To me, what had happened was a catastrophe, but Salvador was looking more and more cheerful.

"Place of ticks, Salvador? What do you mean?"

He leaned back his head and laughed, "That's what Cahal Pech means."

"No!" I said. "Truly?"

"I don't know if it's true. It's the name of some ruins not far away, so Papá Pablo used to say. I am growing to hate this house as much as he ever did."

I didn't tell him how much I loved Doña Catalina, and the house on Avenue Cahal Pech. He put his hands around my shoulders, and pressed me closely against him. "You can tell Rufina about it, if you like. I'll see you in the morning after breakfast."

"Where are you going now, Salvador?" I was alarmed, and anxious to hear what had been discussed. He looked at his watch. "Andrés and I are having dinner at Luis's house. We'll probably stay there overnight."

After I had watched him walk to Luis's black car parked on the driveway, I went into the kitchen to help Rufina prepare a small meal for Doña Catalina.

Although I would never have dreamed of agreeing to go with him to Luis's house, I had hoped Salvador would invite me. It was only a silly wish on my part. I can be impractical sometimes. It's a habit, hard to break.

As I heated the clear broth in a small pot, I tried to explain to Rufina what was happening. She only nodded: perhaps she already knew. The thought that Doña Catalina was upstairs on the *galeria* and that I couldn't join her as I used to do became more and more painful. Rufina took up her tray.

I drank glass after glass of water, trying to drown the pain. Rufina was gone for a while. When she returned I was seated at the kitchen table, my face hidden in my arms. I couldn't stop crying.

Rufina ignored me for a few minutes, then she went out into the garden and picked a cluster of jasmine which she pinned to one side of my hair. The sweet-scented air around my face brought back memories of the night I had first danced with Salvador. "Oh, Rufina. Oh, Rufina," I said.

"It will be fine. Doña Catalina takes advice from Luis. He is in charge of everything as from today."

I lifted my head off the table, thinking of Salvador's anger earlier that afternoon, of his distress and disappointment. Doña Catalina seemed to have resolved the rivalry between Salvador and Andrés by choosing her youngest son to manage the affairs of the estate.

"Do you think, Rufina, that Doña Catalina will come to our wedding?"

"Luis will escort Doña Catalina to your wedding, Luz Marina. The Doña will become reconciled, perhaps when there are children?"

I looked into Rufina's old eyes, grateful for her encouragement. Rufina had aged so much since Don Pablo had left, without sending her even a small message, or a tiny keepsake for his Rufina, such a faithful heart.

And, of course, poor Luis had died that terrible death on the highway, and there had been no wedding, and Doña Catalina has my children, and there can be no reconciliation. Ah, Luis. *Ay Dios*.

Perhaps if Luis had lived, all our lives would have been different. Salvador detested Andrés, but he had always been willing to take the advice of Luis, and of his wife, Maria Elena. I think of Maria Elena, the one woman I believe that Salvador truly respected and loved. Perhaps with her he would have been different than he was with me. The doctor doesn't agree with that idea at all, of course. Perhaps she is right. There is no way for me to know for sure.

However, Salvador became extremely depressed when he discovered that Maria Elena was to marry an American she had met through the Belize Environmental Action Group. The American adopted Luis's children, and they went away, and I don't know if Maria Elena has ever returned to San Joaquín.

My memories, as unreliable as they seem to be at times, have helped me to get through the days in the kitchen garden of Andrés's Caana Hotel. So far I have received eight weekly pay cheques since I started work, but I am no easier in my mind about the Casals and their plans for my children.

Sometimes I see Doña Catalina's silver grey car parked outside Andrés's office. Ducho is usually waiting for her, leaning against the boot of the car as he smokes his cigarettes. Mamá Sofía and I are always very careful to avoid the main hotel lobby, and Andrés's office.

"Maybe tomorrow we can go to town," Mamá Sofía said one morning. She was anxious, like I was, to continue building up the savings we had started, in order to open our own food stall in the plaza. Neither of us could really adjust to the hotel, although the rooms we had been assigned were comfortable.

"Oh, good morning, Señor Andrés," Mamá Sofía called out. Andrés was standing at one of the back windows of the kitchen, looking out at the garden.

"Good morning," he said.

"We haven't seen you of late," Mamá Sofía said. She patted the earth around the pepper plants she was transplanting under the gardener's supervision. "I hope you don't mind if I work sometimes with Luz Marina?"

"Whatever pleases you," Andrés said. Eventually he emerged into the garden as he sometimes did to inspect the lettuce and other vegetables.

As the gardener led Andrés to a greenhouse some distance away, I said to Mamá Sofía, "On Monday the doctor will be at the San Joaquín Hospital. It's time for me to visit her again."

Mamá Sofía was in charge of our savings at the San Joaquín Bank, and she kept careful track of the money we used. "I have enough money in my purse for your bus fare," she said, "and for your prescription. Will you need to buy anything else, Luz Marina?"

I shook my head. "I'll pack my lunch as I usually do."

My doctor, and the probation officer, had not seemed displeased, last month, with my progress. But, of course, I could not bring myself to tell them about my careless outburst at the church barbecue. They did not mention the article in the Belize City newspapers, and this surprised me.

I was still trying to decide whether or not to tell them about the whole thing. I thought I might do that, although it was not to my credit. I learnt very quickly in prison that government officers, like the doctor and the probation officer, and even my lawyer, didn't always tell me everything they knew about my case.

Mamá Sofía was saying, "You're still too thin, Luz Marina. Ask the doctor about it, please? And why do you wear the same shirt and pants day after day?"

Andrés and Hector were walking back so I didn't need to reply to Mamá Sofía's questions. I lifted the wheelbarrow and rolled it nearer to the manure. My shoulders ached, but I knew I would get used to it. A few minutes afterwards the gardener came over to me and said, "You shouldn't be lifting that heavy wheelbarrow, Luz Marina. It's against the hotel rules." Hector smiled in an approving way.

He liked us and I wondered if he knew our history. I doubted it for he lived a solitary life. He ate his meals sitting on one of the benches where he afterwards stretched out for a nap, his hat over his face, his hands folded on his chest. But Mamá Sofía knew about him.

"We must be very careful when we are working with Hector, Luz Marina," she told me in the rooms after our first day.

"Oh, why?" I asked, thinking of the patient way in which he had shown me how to transplant the seedlings. The gardener bit his underlip as he worked, reminding me of Papá Apolonio when he was thinking about something important.

"Well, Luz," she replied, throwing diced onions and garlic into a frying pan, while I tasted the beans stewing on the back burner. It was a treat to be able to cook on a gas stove instead of a fire hearth. "I don't want you to take this the wrong way, but the gardener was in prison once. I am not sure, but I think he is still on probation, like you are."

I looked at my mother in amazement, "For what?"

Mamá Sofía turned her back but I had seen the expression on her face. "Mamá Sofía, did things happen for him, the same way they did for us?"

"Not exactly the same way, of course," Mamá Sofía said. "But some things were similar. Like you, he's trying his best to build a new life. I pretend that I don't know and you must too."

"It's interesting that Andrés put us to work with Hector."

"I agree. But Andrés probably thought it was the best place for us."

"Do you mean because nobody else in the hotel would want to work around me?"

"Maybe that's what he thought."

Just imagine, Luz Marina, I said to myself, throwing more oregano and thyme leaves into a pot of red kidney beans, just think, this is what your life is now. "Jesús!" I said out loud, slamming the spoon down on the stove. I startled my poor Mamá Sofía who looked at me with anxious eyes. I tried to calm myself by carefully lowering the flames under the four large pots bubbling on the gas stove.

On Wednesday morning, I watched Andrés and Hector inspecting the garden, and I wondered what else Andrés must be thinking about me. When he was a few yards away from us, Andrés stopped on the paved path leading to the kitchen. He lifted his hand to his eyes to shade them from the sun.

"Señora Sofía, Luz Marina," Andrés called, "how about having lunch with me tomorrow? You can tell me how you are getting on. Hector tells me you have some ideas for the garden."

I did not reply, but Mamá Sofía, sorting good vegetables from bad, stopped for a moment to wipe beads of sweat from her forehead. Then she said, "Tomorrow is Thursday, no?"

Andrés walked over to Mamá Sofía. "One day each week staff members lunch with me, when I am here," he said.

Hector was nodding. "The food from the kitchen is very good," he said.

"In that case," Mamá Sofía said, "we should accept, eh, Luz Marina?"

"Thank you very much," I said, wishing I was in a position to refuse.

At twelve o'clock the following day, Mamá Sofía and I turned up on the staff veranda, just off the kitchen. Andrés pulled out metal chairs for Mamá Sofía and me. We were still in our working clothes, but we had freshened ourselves up as best as we could in the staff bathroom.

As we sat down, Andrés said, "I approved your request for a day's leave on Monday, Luz Marina."

"Without pay. Thank you, Andrés. I need to visit the doctor." I looked outdoors at the sprays of butter-yellow orchids spilling over the huge branches of a towering tree.

"Only because the court has ordered her to do this, of course," Mamá Sofía said.

"Nothing will be deducted from your pay for medical leave, Luz Marina," Andrés said. "Get the doctor, or whoever it is, to sign the form."

I nodded, and Mamá Sofía said, "I was telling Hector we should plant a lot more *cilantro* for your salads, Andrés."

"An excellent idea, Señora."

The day is humid, like most days during the rainy season. I feel confused, exhausted by the heat. I listen as Mamá Sofía, trying to disguise her nervousness, compliments Andrés on the cold avocado soup, "I couldn't make it better myself, Andrés."

"My staff sometimes contribute their knowledge to the menus. We discuss these things at our lunches."

"Delicious," Mamá Sofía says to Andrés, who smiles, baring his teeth at her. He can't really smile, never could. I feel that he has another reason other than kindness for bringing us to the hotel. I wonder if it has anything to do with my children.

Maybe he thinks he has me in a trap, in his grasp, where he can take his revenge for Salvador's death by watching me squirm and fidget; break my back even, trying to keep my job. I feel sure he knows that on Saturday evenings Mamá Sofía and I travel by bus to the plaza to sell the food we cook in our rooms. Perhaps such thoughts are all "pure fantasy", as Salvador used to call them.

I am trying to distract myself from these thoughts by thinking of the books Doña Catalina and I read together, during that first year. I am sure she reads to Teresa and Eduardo. Poor Feliciano just lies in his crib. What a job Rufina and her new helper must have, shifting Feliciano to different positions several times each day. They are assisting him with gentleness and love, I feel sure.

There was one book Doña Catalina really liked, about people in Europe, Paris or London perhaps, who sat at restaurant tables quite regularly saying intelligent, funny things to each other. She had explained many of the jokes to me and we had laughed and laughed, Doña Catalina and I.

"*Precioso*, no?" Doña Catalina would say, delicately wiping the tears from the corners of her eyes. "What a life it must be, Luz Marina."

"*Si*, Doña," I would reply, thinking how lucky I was to be sitting with her on the *galeria* instead of planting in a *milpa* under the burning sun, or working long hours in a shop for poor pay, as a number of my old school friends did.

Perhaps I should join the library in San Joaquín; perhaps I am well enough now to be able to concentrate on my reading again.

I was thinking these things when I heard Andrés mention Salvador's name and I watched Mamá Sofía put her spoon down. Her napkin dropped to the floor, and Andrés picked it up and gave it to her.

"As I was saying, Señora Sofía, Salvador was my brother but he did not often treat me like one. It never stopped him from destroying my family life."

"Yes," Mamá Sofía said, "I know, it was a great sorrow to you, everybody agrees about that. Forgive me for asking, but where is your wife now?"

"She lives in Belize City. Poor Lydia believed that Salvador loved her. The children sometimes visit me here, of course. But they go about their own business."

"With a little help from their Papá?"

I looked at Mamá Sofía in amazement. I had never seen her like this before. She was sitting upright, her eyes grateful and compassionate as she listened to Andrés. She patted his hand.

"Always, Señora Sofía, with a little help from their Papá. But they don't care too much for me, you know? They try to hide their true feelings, of course." Andrés bared his teeth again, passing a basket of rolls to Mamá Sofía.

"Who knows?" he went on. "I think they have adopted their mother's feelings towards me, which are not always as cordial as I would like."

Andrés laughed as he said these things. Like his father, Don Pablo, he loved to laugh, although from experience I knew that his laugh usually disguised other feelings. Like Don Pablo, Andrés enjoyed lingering over meals, making jokes, exchanging information. From experience, I knew he could be quite hypocritical, but Mamá Sofía seemed completely enchanted.

Andrés's face was the colour of ground white corn. His nose was broad, and above his lips, of a curious thickness, was a sleek moustache, which he smoothed continuously as he talked.

Perhaps he liked to show off his hands, slender and well groomed.

The odour of his aftershave lotion was offensive to me. It reminded me of the night I found him waiting in my room at Doña Catalina's, and of other times when I smelt it before I saw him waiting to talk with me in the garden at night. Salvador had soon put a stop to that practice.

One late afternoon, Andrés had cornered me in the laundry room, off the kitchen, standing with his back against the door. "Why do you humiliate me like this, Luz Marina?"

I stood with the basket of clean clothes in my hand, staring at the white tiles beneath my feet. "Perhaps it is your fate in life, Andrés, to love women who don't love you." I believed, then, that it was only a game to him, *a pasatiempo*, as we say in San Joaquín.

"Especially beautiful ones," Andrés replied, opening the door to let me go through. "You are cruel to me, Luz Marina, when I want to be kind to you."

Maybe he meant, in his way, to be kind then. Who knows now?

Sometimes I don't think Andrés would have noticed me at all if Salvador had not started paying me so much attention; asking me to do this or that favour for him in Andrés's hearing. One morning as they were leaving for the estate office, Andrés said to me, "You'd never do that for me, Luz Marina." His voice was full of reproach. I shrugged.

"Do what for you?" Salvador asked, "Don't tell me you've misplaced your papers, too? Ask her, she'll find them for you."

"Never mind," Andrés said, giving me a baleful look as he and Salvador went with their briefcases through the garden door.

I moved a slice of grilled barracuda around and around on my plate, trying to distract myself by listening to the music and to the voices of the workers in the kitchen, but it was not possible.

"He was my brother," Andrés was saying, looking directly at me, "but I can understand what must have happened that night. How terrible for you."

Mamá Sofía's eyes were shiny, blank, terrified that Andrés would question us about the events surrounding Salvador's death. At that moment I was not frightened any more. I felt angry, determined to say nothing that would in any way incriminate Mamá Sofía and me. I was wondering if Andrés had a tape recorder. In prison I had heard of such things.

"I hope my visits to the doctor and the probation officer will not inconvenience you?" I asked. "I also need to do community service through the church. Right now the women's group is visiting people who are ill and unable to leave their homes."

Andrés was quiet for a minute. Then he said, "Of course not. By the way, I had a visit from your probation officer. It seems as though you will need to be a very good girl for a very long time." He looked at me and grinned.

At Doña Catalina's, I had tried to hide the fact that Andrés sometimes gave me the shudders. I was ashamed of my distaste for him, but I suspect that Doña Catalina knew how I felt, for I was seldom asked to do very much on his behalf.

Except for Don Pablo, the other members of the Casal family treated me well in those first days, but Andrés tried to make sure I was kept in my place. For many months, he referred to me as "the *chapa*" or "the girl" or "the maid". It still felt strange to hear him speak my name.

During those past weeks at the Caana Hotel, he had not been scornful or dismissive, which apparently had lulled Mamá Sofía into a sense of security. But I expected his bad temper and arrogance to flare up at any time.

"My driver and I," Andrés was saying, "are going to be in San Joaquín on Monday. Perhaps we could give you a ride there and back?"

"Perhaps," I said, forcing a smile.

"Well, let the office know what you decide, Luz Marina."

"I'll do that. But sometimes I leave shortly after six o'clock so that I can be first in line at the doctor's office. By eight the hospital is already crowded."

"We leave early ourselves," Andrés said. He drank from a glass of water. "Anything more for you, Señora?"

"No, thank you," Mamá Sofía said, turning to me. "Luz, it would save you getting up so early. These buses are so crowded."

I could feel the pressure mounting. It was almost as though Mamá Sofía had decided to ally herself with Andrés. This was very unsettling to me. I could not risk losing another job so soon. At this rate, when would I ever be able to show the court that I was able to provide for my children?

I conquered my feelings of revulsion as Andrés touched my shoulders familiarly. "Relax, Luz Marina. Nobody is going to bite you." He flashed his teeth at me. He turned to Mamá Sofía. "Do you believe me, Señora, when I say that right at this very moment I feel closer to you, and to Luz Marina, than I feel towards my own family?"

"*Ay, Dios,*" I prayed silently.

"Is that true?" Mamá Sofía asked. "Everybody in your family?"

"Yes, it is true," Andrés said. "My troubles started when Luis was born. I became an extra, only rarely needed."

"Jesús, look at my cross," I prayed quietly, keeping my eyes on Mamá Sofía who was giving Andrés her full attention.

"Papá Pablo treated me badly although I worked so hard. The only thing he ever did for me was to allow me to manage this hotel with my brother, Luis. I must say I was surprised then. He never showed much affection for me."

"And now you are alone, Andrés," Mamá Sofía said, crumbling a roll between her fingers.

"Believe me, Señora Sofía, these experiences have changed me. I am a different person. I am independent now, but growing old." He touched the top of his head delicately. "There is much in my life that I regret."

Mamá Sofía patted his hand again. "Nobody is all bad, Andrés. And look at all you have done, in spite of everything, for Luz Marina and for myself. She joins me in thanking you for your kindness."

"Thank you for those kind words, Señora. They mean a lot to me, coming as they do from you. And Luz Marina, let me know tomorrow if we can give you a ride to San Joaquín," Andrés said. "I am happy to help."

"Yes, Andrés," I replied.

"Shall we go?" He kept his hand firmly under Mamá Sofía's elbow as we walked outside to go back to our rooms. I left my mother there to rest while I went back to work.

At Andrés's Caana Hotel, I woke before light on Friday, in the room I shared with Mamá Sofía. She was already awake, sitting in a low wooden armchair, saying her rosary quietly. I still felt resentful, but I remained silent and went to the tiny indoor bathroom. It was a luxury to shower frequently, which I always needed to do. There was always so much dirt to remove; I can never feel clean enough.

After my bath, I went to the kitchen to get the scissors we used to cut up the plantain leaves in which we boiled *tamales* for sale.

In the bathroom, I did something I thought I would never do. I cut my hair as short as I could. From my bag I removed a bottle of yellow hair dye I'd purchased in the hotel gift shop.

I poured the dye over my hair, rubbed it in, and waited the necessary amount of time before washing it again. In prison I had studied hairdressing, and used to help other female prisoners with their hair. I wasn't very good at it, though.

Wrapping a towel around my head, I went to the kitchen table. As we drank our tea, my mother said, "Why is the towel so stained?"

"I dyed my hair," I said, "and cut it short."

Mamá Sofía crossed herself and muttered, "Jesús, everyone loved your hair."

"It's too hot, all that hair. It gets in the way when I work." I removed the towel.

"My God," my mother said. "You look like a man! Where is the hair?"

I gathered up the long strands and put them in a paper bag. Mamá Sofía took the bag from my hands, went outside and buried it in the bushes. She believed that our enemies could harm me if they possessed hair from my head. On her return, she looked at me strangely.

"How are you feeling, Luz Marina?" She seemed a little frightened by my actions.

"Fine."

"You didn't like your hair any more?"

"I didn't like myself in my hair. I am not that person any more."

"I haven't cut my hair," Mamá Sofía said, "or dyed my hair. Why should you?"

"Who knows?"

"Well," she said, leaning her head to one side, "it doesn't look all that bad."

I shrugged, picked up the towel and walked into the bedroom. Mamá Sofía followed, watching as I began to dress. She sat in her chair, concern in her eyes.

"Thanks to you, things are better for us now. You've sacrificed much, Luz Marina, ever since you were a young girl. It's time to stop now. Don't be so angry. Accept the help we are getting. It may be a gift from God."

"Or from the devil, and I am not angry."

"I don't blame you for your anger. You have a right to it, but it will destroy you."

"I am not hurting anybody."

"But you will, if you're not careful. We must both be careful. You don't pray any more, Luz Marina?"

"It's hard to pray, but I pray."

At four o'clock that afternoon, I went to collect my pay. I stood in line feeling unclean, even though I had washed again before entering the office. I felt defensive, guilty and ashamed all the time. I was so tired of feeling this way.

Each time I tried to make a small atonement, something happened and I destroyed it. Perhaps I should be more humble, more open, more everything. I had lost trust in myself, and in Mamá Sofía, which for me was a lonely place. The very worst was the feeling of being naked, without cover.

I was glad that I had cut my hair and dyed it. It gave the office staff an excuse to stare at me openly, instead of averting their eyes in my presence. Perhaps if I looked as ugly as I felt, they would feel they could dismiss me from their thoughts.

The knots in my stomach were terrible as I folded my week's pay and slipped it into my bag. I sat on a chair in the office until the secretary told me to go in to see Andrés.

The look on his face when he saw my hair was a little comical. I had to smile in spite of the seriousness of my situation, and my nervousness.

"I wouldn't have recognised you on the street," he said. A stack of cheques was on one side of the desk. An open chequebook was before him.

"A small moment, Luz Marina." He continued to sign the cheques.

Standing on the bookcase behind his desk was a framed photograph of the entire Casal family. It was familiar to me, and I was almost positive it hadn't been there the first time I visited Andrés's office. Don Pablo and Doña Catalina sat in the middle of their various offspring in the photograph. Salvador, the tallest, was looking straight at me, a half-smile on his face. He was dressed, as he always was on formal occasions, in a white, long-sleeved *guayabrera*, open at the neck. His thick black hair was combed back from his forehead. I looked at his nose, straight and narrow; his eyes, deep-set and dark. I heard his voice, caressing, intimate with those he liked or wanted to charm; carelessly offhand with anyone not the immediate focus of his attention.

In the chair beside Andrés's desk, I continued to wait. I did not know what Andrés was thinking now, but I distrusted him as much as I ever had, as I had grown to distrust Salvador. Andrés put his pen down, and I said, "Señor Andrés, my recent experiences have not left me. I am not well."

"Call me Andrés. Why have you started this Señor business again? You are like family."

I wondered why he looked so confident, so in charge, so sure. Perhaps it was because of the jobs he gave to people like me. What power he had. What must it be like? Andrés was tough, sly under his gentlemanly cover, like Salvador had been.

"I want to be open and honest, if you will forgive me," I said to Andrés. "I am grateful for this job. Mamá Sofía and I, we try to give extra hours to the garden, to show our gratitude. But there is a limit to how much I can pay. Do you understand?"

He lowered his lashes, waiting to see if I would continue. As I well knew, this was another one of his snares. He would listen until you betrayed yourself. He would lead a person into excess.

I hesitated, then said, "I am not sure it would be right to accept your offer."

"Oh, but why not?" He laughed playfully. "I am always looking out for your welfare, but you don't trust me. You've never given me a chance to show you how nice I can be!"

The telephone rang, and he picked it up. "What time did you say you wanted to be at the hospital, Luz Marina?"

I thought of my children, and of Mamá Sofía, and realised that perhaps I should not continue risking my job by further antagonising Andrés. "Is seven o'clock too early, Andrés?"

"That's perfect," Andrés said, cradling the telephone against his ear and leafing through his chequebook. "See you on Monday."

In gaol I had heard of certain inmates who, after their release, committed crimes, small and large, in order to be sent back to prison. They had lost the ability, or the will, to live outside. Until that moment, I had never understood how anyone could feel this way.

On Saturday, thunder wakes me before light. It sounds as though a mountain is falling through the roof; my heart beats wildly. Lightning is flashing through the windows, and I can see the trees bending in the high wind. There will be no work in the garden until the weather clears. I dress, and remove a raincoat and an umbrella from the hooks near the door. I sit in a chair, my chin in my hand, waiting for the office to open at nine o'clock.

"Aren't you going to have something to eat, Luz Marina?" Mamá Sofía calls to me from our kitchen where she is drinking tea, and eating a sweet roll with melted cheese.

"I'm not hungry. I am going to the office."

"In this weather? Why don't we start on the food to sell in the plaza tomorrow?"

"I'm going to tell Andrés that we're leaving – at least, I'm leaving."

She appears in the doorway, wiping her hand on a dish towel, a look of fear rising in her eyes.

"We are just getting comfortable here, Luz. Why?"

"I can see that you are comfortable, Mamá. But I am not. Maybe Andrés will allow you to stay since you seem to like each other."

"What do you mean? I do my very best to be polite, friendly to Andrés for the sake of the children, and for our sakes, too. But I don't like him, not at all."

"I thought I was free, Mamá Sofía, when the judge said to me, 'I will not keep you in prison one minute more.'"

"That's only natural. You were there for so long. But I don't think we can ever be free again, Luz Marina."

"No. I can see that we will have to serve more, if different, time, in service to Andrés Casal."

"How can we run for ever, Luz Marina? We have to be humble, accept what is offered. Think of Perla. She has her faults but she is trying to be sensible. She knows that she has to sacrifice certain things to obtain others. Don't you want your children?"

"Yes."

"You are not a young girl any more. There is no reason for us to spend the rest of our days sleeping on the cold cement in the plaza."

Mamá Sofía removes the raincoat and the umbrella from my hands. "Think of your children, Luz Marina. Don't you want what's best for them? Be careful or you might lose them entirely.

Do you think I don't care about you and about Feliciano, Teresa and Eduardo?"

"I know you do, Mamá Sofía."

"This whole thing has made you so cold, Luz Marina. I can hardly recognise your spirit."

"Sometimes I can hardly recognise myself."

I lie across the bed, listening to the rain, staring at the trees, thinking of my children, except for poor Feliciano, playing happily on a day like today under the shelter of Doña Catalina's *galeria*. Perhaps they have already forgotten me.

On our return from San Joaquín, Andrés had said, "I'd like to visit you and your mother later this evening. Is that all right?"

"Yes," I said, getting out of the car and going towards our rooms to change for work. I was still thinking about what the doctor at the hospital had said.

The visit to the doctor in the morning, and working in the kitchen garden until late afternoon, left me feeling drained. After nightfall, I sat in a chair in the corner of the veranda outside our rooms waiting with some apprehension for Andrés to arrive. The moon was full, shining on the rooftops of the cottages scattered about the hotel grounds.

Although I had arrived early, people were already crowding into the waiting room. I took the first seat outside the doctor's office until she arrived.

"Good morning, Luz Marina," she said, walking towards me, jingling her keys. "Come right in."

"Good morning, Doctor," I said, following her into the office. She turned on the two overhead fans and tilted the green blinds. A number of files were on the desk.

I knew she must recently have arrived from Belize City or from seeing other patients on the wards, but she looked as if she'd just arrived from home. She wore navy blue shoes, stockings, and a white coat over a pretty navy dress, with white polka dots, and tiny pearl buttons down the front.

"Tell me your secret," I wanted to say. "Tell me how to have more control over what happens in my life." But, nice as she was, the doctor did not have too much patience with that kind of talk, or with too long a silence. I swallowed; my throat ached.

She didn't comment on my bright yellow hair, which was too long in the front and much too short at the back. Mamá Sofía said the back of my hair looked like ruffled fowl feathers.

"Luz, you've changed jobs, I see." She was examining my file. She spoke softly, but I was aware of the watch on her slender wrist.

"I lost my job, my other job. It was all I could find." I looked down at my hands. The nails were short, broken in places, but they were absolutely clean.

"I can't imagine that it is easy for you to be working at the Caana. It has to be more than a little disturbing."

"It's not easy," I said, trying to memorise the jauntiness in her speech. Its undertone suggested that an effort should be made. "But I am trying to make some headway in this new life."

Dr Marjorie Anne tapped her lined yellow pad with her pen. "At the Caana Hotel, Luz Marina?" She wore a plain gold ring with a small diamond which I had not seen before. Perhaps she was engaged to be married.

I didn't like to think about what Dr Marjorie Anne would imagine if I told her that Andrés Casal and his driver had brought me to the hospital. I think the doctor believes that I can be a sensible person, and I am trying hard to be.

"I seem to have this idea of who I was, who I should be. I do want to be something like that again. I don't want to serve in a bar, places like that, going further down all the time."

The doctor frowned at my files and did not reply.

I swallowed and began crying, thinking of the precious moments I was wasting, of the people sitting on the chairs outside her door.

She crossed the room and filled a tumbler with water from an aluminium jug, tinkling with ice cubes. She handed it to me. I drank a little, setting it down carefully on the desk, which was covered with a large sheet of glass.

I blew my nose several times into my handkerchief, not wanting to look at her, wishing I could bring myself to even think about what she wanted to discuss.

I heard Andrés's footsteps on the concrete walk. I was glad it was dark because he couldn't see my expression. I could sense his mood. He sat in the chair beside me. Mamá Sofía did not come outside. I heard the hiss of the onions and garlic. I was glad that I was not alone with Andrés.

I didn't really listen as he told me how sorry he was for me, and how I deserved a better life, how he had always loved me. With Andrés, one rarely knew what his true feelings were. He lifted my hand to his lips.

"I want you to live with me, Luz, then you wouldn't have to work so hard. Soon, I'll be a rich man. We'll have a wonderful life together."

"Aren't you rich now?" I stared over the veranda railings, down the path to the cottages strung out row after row, the outdoor lights glowing.

"Not like I want to be. If the land deal comes off – and if I have anything to say, it will – I'll build a couple more hotels with the money." His hands were around my shoulders.

"Perhaps you will succeed, Andrés." He kissed my cheek lightly. His kiss was wet.

"Then I'll be free of my mother," he said. "I'll be able to purchase her shares if she agrees to sell. If not, it doesn't matter. I'll be away at another hotel, and put a manager here. I'd like you to share in this, live with me."

"I couldn't do that," I said.

He lit a cigar, smoking for a while before resting it in the ashtray on the table beside his chair.

"You lived with our family before. You were happy. You know how we are. I would protect you." His hands were around my waist, moving over my body.

"I am sorry, Andrés, I can't."

"You are ungrateful, Luz Marina." He was trying to kiss my lips, so I got out of the chair and went to stand in the doorway. Mamá Sofía stood at the kitchen door. Our eyes met. Hers were anguished. I don't know what she could have seen in my own, except horror and fear.

"I don't feel ungrateful, Andrés. Let me think about it overnight." At the kitchen door, Mamá Sofía was nodding. "I need to discuss this with my mother."

"Of course. She has to be involved. Let me know what you decide in the morning. Promise?" He was trying his best to smile, to appear reassuring, but I feel sure he was offended.

"I will let you know in the morning, Andrés."

At about eleven o'clock the following day, I entered the door of the hotel office, glad to be out of the wind and rain. Outside, the trees were bending over as if they would touch the ground. The wind was violent, the trees thrashing about. The cottages were silent. The office was quiet, with many employees kept away from work by the inclement weather.

I went up to the clerk's desk, hearing my feet squelching in my wet and muddy shoes. My face was streaming with water, and the clerk offered me a box of paper tissues. I wiped my hands and my face, leaving the dripping umbrella in a corner. I removed my raincoat and said I had an appointment with Señor Andrés Casal.

The clerk indicated a chair and I sat down, while he dialled the number. "You can go in," he said.

Andrés's secretary brought in coffee. I held it in my hands but I didn't drink it.

"Andrés," I said as soon as she left, "I would like us to be friends. I would like to continue working here."

He came around the desk to where I sat and began smoothing down my hair. "Don't do that, please, Andrés."

"But why? Think about it, Luz Marina. If we are together, we can get your children from my mother."

"What about your own children?"

"My wife will not let me have them. It's better for them to be with their mother. I want to start a new life."

"How will you treat my children?"

"Like my own, of course; they are my blood relatives."

"I can't."

"I am too ugly?" He looked at the picture of his family on the wall. "Salvador would expect me to take care of you. Luis as well."

"I don't want to get into that kind of life again. It is unsafe for me. Salvador scorned me for living with him."

"I wouldn't scorn you."

"So you say now."

"I wouldn't, Luz, not if you open your heart to me."

This was what I feared that I could not do. He held me in his arms but I kept my clenched fist between us, wondering what to do. I was thinking of the future of my children who were Casals too. "Supposing I can't, can't ..."

"Make love to me? It will happen. I will make you want it to happen."

The secretary opened the door, then tried to close it again. Behind her stood Doña Catalina, her face rigid with shock. I made to leave the room, but she was already inside the doorway. She did not acknowledge my presence.

"We need to talk in private," she said to Andrés.

"Have a seat, Madre," Andrés said.

"No, thank you. I'm not staying." She glanced around the room as though I wasn't there. My feet were muddy, my clothes wet, and I was conscious that I smelled like stale tortillas.

"I'll wait in the conference room. The secretary tells me the meeting is scheduled for one o'clock. Why did you ask me to get here so early?" Her eyes were bright, as if with tears, her voice quavering with distress.

Andrés rose from his desk and went to where she was standing. "Luz and I are thinking of living together, maybe even getting married. We are hoping that you will let us have Feliciano, Teresa and Eduardo."

"You should be thinking of your own children, not Salvador's. They are my responsibility, as he would have wanted." She was speaking to me as well, I knew.

"If we are living together or married, the courts will agree that we can have the children. My wife left me. I did not send her away."

"If you divorce your wife to live with or marry the person who caused Salvador's death, don't expect to receive a single *centavo* from me when I die."

"What I have is enough, Madre. I am grateful."

"Tell me exactly what it is that you think you have?" Doña Catalina's voice was very soft, she held herself erect, although I noticed she still used her silver-headed cane.

Andrés was taken aback and looked at her as if thunderstruck. "This hotel, and the land, which Padre and yourself so generously gave to me. I hope to sell some of the land, as you know. We've discussed it together."

"I have never transferred the title of this land to you." She lifted her cane and pointed through the window.

"A formality, I know that. I'd be grateful if you would do so, Madre, as you've promised."

"I will wait to see how things work out between you and your wife, and with me. Your father would find your actions too incredible for words."

"He always did," Andrés said, trying to laugh, "and you too, Madre."

"I am warning you, Andrés."

My tongue seemed stuck to the roof of my mouth. I was shivering, but my skin burned. Doña Catalina turned back and walked through the door.

White as a sheet, Andrés followed her, and I heard him say, "Give me a chance to discuss this further with you, Madre. We have always been able to work out these matters of business."

"I agree," Doña Catalina said. "The business should be our first priority." I felt sure she meant me to hear her words.

How that Tuesday passed, I am not sure. Mamá Sofía and I spent most of the day discussing what had happened in Andrés's office. As we thought about packing up once again, Mamá Sofía prayed audibly for the skies to clear so that we could sell the food she had prepared the evening before.

By afternoon the rain had stopped, and we returned to work in the kitchen garden. As we raked and weeded, Mamá Sofía said, "Maybe we should just leave now. I doubt if anyone would notice."

"I'm not sneaking away, Mamá Sofía. We'll wait until Friday, and I'll collect my wages. We've worked for it."

That night was humid and depressing. The world seemed waterlogged and dreary. Mamá Sofía and I went to bed early, although we did not sleep. We talked to each other in the darkness or stared at the fireflies massing on the screened windows. I must have dozed a little, because some time later Mamá Sofía was shaking my shoulders.

"Andrés is here, Luz Marina. He's in the outside room."

I looked at the clock. It was about ten. Getting out of bed, I pulled on some clothes, slipped my feet into my shoes and went into the other room. I pulled my shawl around my shoulders, for I felt as though I had caught a cold.

Andrés's car was parked outside, but no driver sat in it. I guessed he did not want too many people to know that he was visiting us.

"Please don't get up," I said. I knew that he was not here merely to ask us to leave. The office could do that.

"Hello, Luz Marina, my apologies for visiting you so late." He looked at the empty boxes I had placed against the wall nearest the door. "You are leaving, I see."

"Unless you think I can keep my job, Andrés. Do you want us to continue?"

"Forgive me, but my mother insists that you leave. I would like to offer you some small compensation."

"What kind of compensation?" Mamá Sofía said, rocking back and forth in a chair. "You told us we were like your family. Now you want to get rid of us."

Andrés's face closed in. His eyes looked glazed. He spoke with difficulty. "You still feel like my family, Señora. This is why I would like to offer you a gift to enable you to make a fresh start."

He drew an envelope from the pocket of his jacket and counted out ten hundred-dollar bills. I could see no trace of the man who a short time ago had asked me to live with him. He placed the money on the small table in the centre of the room.

"My mother and I had a long discussion this afternoon," he said. "I am convinced that she needs my help and co-operation. In addition, I have a number of financial obligations."

"That is quite natural," Mamá Sofía said.

"But it is not easy for me, Señora. As I told you and Luz Marina, I had hoped to change my life. That was the truth."

"Do you know if Doña Catalina is willing to allow me to see my children?" I asked.

"At least, occasionally," Mamá Sofía added. "She can grant us that gift, if she wishes, I believe."

"To be truthful," Andrés said to us, "my mother and I did not discuss the children. She is hoping, I believe, to adopt them legally. After that has been done, I am sure visiting rights would not be a problem."

"Please inform Doña Catalina that I cannot give up my children."

"My mother, I am sure, would want to offer you a suitable compensation. She is willing to do whatever is necessary for the best interests of Feliciano, Teresa and Eduardo. She loves them very much."

To me, his words seemed like a warning.

He stood up, his hands in his pockets, rocking back and forth on his heels. "I tried to do what I could. As you saw today, Luz Marina, my situation permits me to go no further."

"You are powerless?" Mamá Sofía said, a slight smile on her face.

"I may be, Señora, I may indeed be, for the time being, in any case."

I replaced the money in the envelope and returned it to him. "I will collect whatever is owed to me from the office, Andrés."

"As you wish, Luz Marina." His face was red with embarrassment and frustration. We sat in silence for several minutes, then he said goodnight and left.

Mamá Sofía and I avoided each other's eyes for the next few minutes. She sat hunched over in the rocking chair, staring at the cement floor.

"We've tried so hard and they win every time," I said, going to the kitchen to make us both some coffee. It was not likely we would sleep again that night. I had decided to be finished with our packing before morning.

"We've saved a little," Mamá Sofía said. "Things could be worse. Maybe we have enough money now to be able to get a licence for the stall in the plaza?"

"We can try, Mamá Sofía," I said, thinking with longing of my old job and our rooms on the Elodio Alpuche Guerra *rancho*.

On the last day we spent at Andrés's Caana Hotel, Mamá Sofía received a long letter from Perla, enclosing a little money. "Perla says she is planning another visit to us soon," Mamá Sofía said. "We can send a little of this to poor Concha. She is so brave."

"Yes, Mamá Sofía," I said, tying up our boxes with yellow plastic twine, trying not to think of Concha's big light brown eyes, wide with terror on the evening of Salvador's death. I forced myself to remember her deep dimples, her mischievous smile, her trust in me when we were young girls on our old *milpa* with Mamá Sofía and Papá Apolonio.

Part 4

As usual Mamá Sofía and I woke up early in the bed we shared in the tiny room to the rear of our café. I stared up at the zinc roof for a moment, uncertain of the time, and of where I was. Now that we were working here in the Plaza San Joaquín, I thought a lot about my Papá Apolonio, and about Salvador. Perhaps it was the knowledge that my children were so near.

From our café in the evenings, I was able to see the lights in Doña Catalina's house. Perhaps one day I would see the shadows of Teresa and Eduardo on the window shades, or against the walls of Doña Catalina's red sitting room.

Several weeks ago, in early October, on our visit to the town board, it was a pleasant surprise to discover we had saved enough money to pay something extra to the clerk. He made it easy for us to get our licence and to set up a night and day café, situated almost directly facing Avenue Cahal Pech where Doña Catalina lives.

Through Dolores's knowledge of the second-hand stores, Mamá Sofía and I were able to purchase an old gas stove with an oven. At another shop, Dolores helped us to pick out rickety but still serviceable metal tables and chairs. I also bought a dilapidated plastic awning with several holes. Tomás brought everything to the café in his pick-up truck.

He helped us to set out the tables and chairs, and to hoist the awning, which we had cleaned and patched. Once it was up, the sun shone through the awning, spreading a cool green light over the table and chairs. The colour reminded me of the ferns, vines and mosses on the forest floor where Salvador, the children and I used to walk beneath trees which met high above our heads.

151

We decided to call our small restaurant the Café Feliciano, and paid a young boy to paint a simple sign on the front of the stall.

In the café, we served coffee, tea and the sweet rolls we baked. In the mornings we sold fried eggs, bread, beans and tea. Each afternoon and evening, we offered rice, beans, and some kind of meat. My mother or I had to visit the market almost every day as we had no refrigerator.

The cooking space was small, so we were often in each other's way when we first got started. One morning about nine o'clock when the breakfast rush was over, Mamá Sofía and I decided we would try to increase our sales that day by serving a special meal in the evening. We advertised it on a chalk board in front of the shop.

"Those last chickens we bought from Dolores Gonzalez Paz were tender," Mamá Sofía said. "Buy from her again."

"Now, Mamá Sofía?" I asked, serving sweet buns and hot coffee to two men sitting under the far end of our awning.

"I think so," she said, looking around. "I can handle things until you return." Mamá Sofía gave me some money as I removed the basket from its nail in the kitchen wall. I tied my scarf tightly under my chin, and slipped on my dark glasses.

"You should practise walking in the street without that scarf and those shades, Luz Marina," Mamá Sofía said.

"But Mamá Sofía," I wanted to say, "at least I don't wear them in our café any more," but she knew that. I felt so much better wearing my shades and scarf on the streets; more in control somehow.

On a recent visit to the doctor, she'd said to me, "So how are you doing? Your hair is growing back, I see." I smiled and said to her, "I am learning to live with who I am now." This is true, of course. I just wish I could like this new self as it now seems I did the old.

I was always glad for any excuse to see Dolores again, although she was often so busy with customers that we couldn't talk for very long. While we were preparing to open the café, she and I had talked a little about my old job at the Elodio Alpuche Guerra *rancho*.

"The pastor told me what happened, Luz Marina," she'd said, as we walked through a nearby second-hand store examining cups and saucers for cracks.

"I know," I replied, picking up a plastic container of rusty utensils, selecting forks, spoons and knives.

"Elodio Alpuche Guerra was a little hasty in his actions. That's my opinion." She was counting the pile of saucers and cups on the counter before her.

"Do you really think so, Dolores?" I separated the knives, forks and spoons, trying to decide how many we could afford.

"I do. Tomás was telling me only the other night that Elodio Alpuche Guerra has decided not to sell his land after all. Andrés Casal and Doña Catalina are quite upset, according to Tomás."

"Tomás is very reliable," I said, trying not to think about Doña Catalina and Andrés.

"International pressure is mounting, so Tomás says." We carried a heavy box to the cashier. "The foreign buyers seem to be backing away."

"How many acres do they need to plant in citrus?"

"Oh, who knows? Maybe forty or fifty thousand acres? I've probably got that wrong; a lot, anyway."

"Too much," I replied, trying to imagine it. It was hard. I could only see people in the villages and towns going about their everyday business.

Salvador had been so disappointed that night, long ago now, when Don Pablo had refused to donate land for a park, or perhaps it had been a nature reserve. Sitting with Salvador on the steps outside our house by the river, I tried to console him. "It's not important anyway, Salvador, is it? There's enough bush around for everyone."

Salvador had given me one of his sidelong glances, the ones that told me not to be so ridiculous. "I think you see life too narrowly, Luz Marina," he said, "as does Papá Pablo." Perhaps Salvador was right; it is something to think about.

As I walk towards Dolores's shop to purchase the chickens for our café, the plaza is noisy and bustling. It is usually like this on Saturdays. Vendors are trying to sell me big bunches of balloons or small towers of cotton candy, a bright pink, with streaks of red. I look towards the fountain in the centre of the plaza. Young couples sit on the edges, trailing their hands in the water, just as Salvador and I used to do.

On certain Saturday evenings we would stroll up and down the plaza, sometimes stopping for an ice-cream, or for *panades*, at a stall Salvador liked to patronise. At other times, we would sit on the benches beneath the umbrella-shaped trees listening to the plucking of guitar strings, holding hands as we listened to sad love songs. We seemed to be happy then.

Did we really enjoy each other's company in those early days, as I seem to remember? Today it is very hard for me to believe that we did. Still, the touch of his hand on my shoulders, and the sound of his laugh in my ear, seem quite real in my mind.

By the time I reached the end of the plaza, and turned left into the unpaved lane where Dolores's shop is situated, I was drenched in sweat. Up ahead I saw Dolores outside her shop selling fruits and vegetables to several customers from boxes and baskets piled outside her door.

"Dully, Dullita!" I called to her in my mind as I used to do when we were schoolgirls together. But now I was reluctant to draw attention to myself so I waited until I was next to her before I said hello. Her cheerful face and wide smile gave my spirits a lift.

"Luz Marina," she said. "Just the person I was hoping to see." I waited until she was finished, watching as she gave change from the pockets in the front of her apron.

Dolores's shop was very deceptive. From the street, it seemed modest, an ordinary grocery store. To the rear, however, her husband Tomás managed a small wholesale warehouse. He sold zinc, bales of cloth, mirrors, paper, school supplies and a variety of other things to smaller retail shops.

I drank the glass of cold water Dolores placed in my hands. As she removed the chickens from the freezer and put them in my bag, she asked, "How is business, Luz Marina?"

"Not bad, Dolores," I replied, looking around at the shelves of tinned food, the cheeses in the glass cases and the scale hanging from the ceiling. A customer waited at the cash register to pay for onions, garlic and a small bag of *habanero* peppers.

Overhead, I heard her children running around, and the voice of an older woman urging them to go outside and play in the yard. Dolores nearly always had a variety of relatives staying in her home for shorter or longer periods of time.

"When are you and Tomás going to visit us again?"

"Tonight, Luz Marina, as a matter of fact. We have a visitor from Belize City, somebody we want you to meet."

"Really?" I replied, selecting a dozen small balls of *ricado* spice from a large glass jar on the counter. "Who is it?"

"The new executive secretary of the environmental society. Tomás is taking him around now, meeting different people in San Joaquín."

"We'll be glad to have you as our guests," I said, as she helped me to put potatoes into a blue plastic bag.

"Are you sure, Luz Marina? It's not putting you to any trouble?"

"Positive, Dolores," I replied, feeling a rush of gratitude towards her and Tomás.

On my return to the Café Feliciano, I told Mamá Sofía that Dolores, Tomás and a visitor would be coming to our café as our guests.

"I am glad," Mamá Sofía said. "They have done so much to help us."

As she had promised, Dolores, Tomás and their friend, a tall, middle-aged man with greying hair, turned up at our café that evening shortly after nine o'clock. Most of our regular customers had eaten and left.

"I've heard a lot about you, Miss Figueroa," Carlos Ochoa Palmas said. "I am happy to have this chance to talk with you and Señora Sofía."

"May we be no more strangers," Mamá Sofía replied, as I nodded politely and began serving the chicken, stewed with onions and vegetables.

"This looks delicious, Luz Marina," Tomás said, helping himself from the dishes on the table.

I smiled at Tomás, whose dark eyes under arching eyebrows were very earnest. Dolores once complained to me that Tomás ate twice as much as she did but hardly gained any weight. Tomás regularly encouraged his wife to go on a diet. She often did, but with little success.

"All kinds of people belong to the society," Dolores was saying, "don't they, Carlos?" She arranged lettuce leaves and carrots around her plate before placing a small mound of chicken in the middle.

"Yes, indeed," Carlos Ochoa Palmas replied, helping himself to another tortilla. "Everything is delicious," he said.

As I sat down at the table, Carlos Ochoa Palmas began drinking the coffee Mamá Sofía placed before him. He didn't want any fruit or cake.

"How is Evangelica?" Mamá Sofía asked Dolores, remembering that she was the leader of the women's group at the church.

"Busy as usual, Mamá Sofía. We see Luz Marina regularly, but we miss you at the services."

"One of these days I'll pay Evangelica a surprise visit," Mamá Sofía said. "But I hold down the fort here when Luz Marina has work to do there."

Carlos Ochoa Palmas removed a handkerchief from his pocket, patted his mouth and said, "We are planning to start a weekly radio programme in the near future."

"Excellent idea," Tomás said. "The society used to have one years ago, but it went off the air for some reason or other."

Carlos Ochoa Palmas drew a newspaper clipping from his briefcase and said apologetically, "I am wondering, Luz Marina, whether you would mind doing an interview, as one of the guests, on our programme?" He pushed the clipping towards me but I did not pick it up.

"Is that the article about the land deal?" Tomás asked. Both Dolores and he looked a little embarrassed.

Carlos Ochoa Palmas nodded and Mamá Sofía gave a little cough.

"I am sorry but I am not able to do an interview at this time, Señor," I said. I shook the hair away from my forehead and smiled, trying not to remember that meeting with Doña Catalina at Señor Elodio's office.

Señor Ochoa Palmas did not seem surprised. He replaced the clipping in his briefcase. "Here's my card," he said. "Please let me know if you change your mind."

"We would like to join the society, of course," Mamá Sofía said. "But our café keeps us busy. Perhaps at a later date."

"At least come with Tomás and me to one of the meetings," Dolores said to Mamá Sofía and myself. "You wouldn't regret it, I promise."

"Sure, Dolores, just let me know when," I said, looking at Mamá Sofía, who nodded and said, "Of course, Dolores."

A few days later I was serving customers at the tables when a well-dressed man asked to speak with me. When I asked him what he wanted, he said, "I am from the Ministry of Health and I am here to inspect the premises. We do this every now and then."

He showed me his identification and I lifted part of the counter, which is on hinges. He stepped into our stall, bumping his feet on the two aluminium buckets in which we wash the cups, saucers and other things.

The inspector pushed aside the curtain separating the stall from our bedroom. "This is your residence?" His tone was very unfriendly. I thought of asking him to have a free meal at our café later that evening, but I wasn't sure he was the kind of person who could be swayed by that kind of invitation.

So I nodded, waiting as he walked around the small space, making notes in his book. I tried to control my annoyance. Mamá Sofía was outside serving the few customers we had at this time of the day.

"Lots of flies," he said, looking at the cooking area. He stepped to the rear of the stall. "Why don't you get some covers for your garbage cans?"

"We have covers," I said. "Here they are."

He covered the garbage cans which had recently been emptied. He made a note of the string mop standing in dirty water. After he had completed his inspection, Mamá Sofía gave him some tea, but he insisted on paying for it.

The inspector sat under the green awning slowly sipping his tea as he looked around. We continued serving at the tables, trying to ignore his presence. When he left, about an hour later, he seemed no friendlier than before.

The following week we received a letter telling us that we had failed the inspection and giving us instructions on what to do in order to keep our licence. The letter suggested that we install running water, and purchase garbage cans with tight-fitting lids. We were also to remove all cardboard boxes which constituted a fire hazard.

We resolved to do these things as soon as we had the money and time. There were many other stalls like ours, some with even fewer amenities than we had, so Mamá Sofía and I didn't think too much about the matter until one day the food inspector appeared again. He told us not to reopen the café until the requirements had been met.

"A lot of stall owners don't have running water," Mamá Sofía complained.

"We get to everyone, in due course," the inspector said.

Feeling defeated, Mamá Sofía and I closed the café and went to visit Dolores at about five o'clock. Her grocery store wouldn't open again until about seven that evening. We sat in Dolores's tiny office to the rear of her shop and explained our problems with the food inspector.

"Somebody is trying to get to you," Dolores said. "You should try to get some protection. We are always careful to do that."

"What do you suggest, Dolores?" Outside her children and their friends were screaming and laughing as they ran around the yard trying to catch each other. Tomás sat in the shade of a plum tree leafing through a pile of bills.

"If I were you," Dolores said, "I'd talk to somebody like Señor Miguel Rivas. Don't waste any time. He's been known to help people in your situation."

"He's an elected politician, Mamá Sofía," I said to my mother, who didn't remember the name. I thought back to the conversation

I had overheard in Elodio Alpuche Guerra's office. I didn't think Señor Miguel Rivas would be eager to help us at all, but we had to try everything.

"What could he do?" Mamá Sofía asked.

"I'm sure he could get you an extension, at the very least. People do that every day. Miguel Rivas holds a clinic for his constituents on Wednesday afternoons."

After some discussion, Mamá Sofía and I decided we would attend Miguel Rivas's next clinic. Dolores agreed to store our food in the big deep freeze in her shop.

As we were about to leave, she showed Mamá Sofía and me a number of leaflets describing the Belize Environmental Action Group. "Why don't you come with us to the meeting on Monday?" Dolores urged again. "It'll take you at least a few days to get the café opened again."

"We'll try, Dolores, and thanks again," I said.

It was late when we left Dolores's shop to return to the Café Feliciano. In spite of my reservations, Mamá Sofía felt greatly encouraged at the thought that with an extension the café need not be closed for long. In the meantime, we would use our savings to install running water, just to be on the safe side. We couldn't afford to get into any trouble with the government.

As we neared the Plaza San Joaquín, we heard fire engine bells ringing. People were rushing into the plaza from every side and we walked quickly, anxious to be out of the crowd of excited people.

When we reached the area where our stall was located, Mamá Sofía gripped my hand, "It's our café, Luz Marina!" We pushed our way to the front of the crowd. The firemen were spraying water on the fire, but they had arrived far too late. Everything we owned had been destroyed.

Before we went, earlier that afternoon, to Dolores's house we had stored the chairs and folding tables inside the stall. They were twisted and blackened. Someone had tried to save the green plastic awning but it was half-burnt, and a fireman stood on what was left of it pointing his hose towards the smouldering stall.

Our eyes were riveted on the remains of our café. We held hands, and stood silently trying to absorb what had happened. Several policemen were on the scene and one of them said to Mamá Sofía and me, "Your gas tank must have had a leak. It exploded. Be sure to visit the station tonight and make your report."

In confusion, and a desire for some sense of order, Mamá Sofía and I started walking to the police station. We heard someone call, "Luz Marina!" Rufina was hurrying towards us, her shawl pulled tightly down over her forehead.

She seemed dazed. It had been nearly two years since I had last seen her. I looked at her with pleading eyes. She said, "I heard the engines and had a feeling it was your stall!"

Mamá Sofía said, "What would make you feel that way, Rufina? Do you know anything about it?"

Rufina did not seem to hear Mamá Sofía's question, for she turned to me.

"I do my best for your children, Luz Marina. I'll be sorry to see them go."

"Go where, Rufina?" I felt as if I couldn't stand up a moment longer.

"I heard Doña Catalina say something about taking them to the States for a while. She wants to put Feliciano in a special hospital."

"I want so badly to see them, Rufina," I said.

"It is only natural." She looked down at her feet in transparent plastic slippers. "Well, I'd better get back before I'm missed."

"Rufina," I said, gripping her arm tightly. "How is Feliciano?"

"The same, the same, Luz Marina. I'll send you a message, if I can."

Before I could say anything more, Rufina was scurrying away through the crowds. We watched until we could no longer see her thin, white shawl trailing down the back of her dark grey dress with tiny pink flowers.

Feeling distraught, Mamá Sofía and I continued on our way to the San Joaquín police station, the inside of which I had hoped never to see again. We were extremely nervous as we stood beneath the archway of the large cream-coloured building, not far away from the Hawkesworth Bridge over the Río Caracol.

"The owner has insurance on the stall, no?" Mamá Sofía said, as we hesitated outside the station door.

"Who knows? I think we would have smelled the gas if the tank had a leak, Mamá Sofía. We were always on our guard against fires."

Part 5

It was nearly midnight when Mamá Sofía and I rented a room in the boarding house above Nora's Restaurant. Earlier we had spent some time buying a few necessary items in the plaza where most of the shopkeepers seemed sympathetic to us. That night I dreamt about my Papá Apolonio. He seemed unusually elated, his nostrils flaring, his eyes glittering as he walked along the path between the cohune palms towards our old home on the *milpa*.

Papá Apolonio wore his old straw hat, and his machete in its sheath bounced on his hip as it used to do. Drawing Mamá Sofía aside, he whispered in her ear, shooing Perla and Concha away.

"Is that true, Apolonio?" Mamá Sofía was asking, her voice high with disbelief.

In my dream, I watched my sisters chasing a hen and her brood of yellow chickens into the ramshackle coop to one side of our house.

Papá Apolonio was laughing with happiness as he pushed his hat to the back of his head.

In my dream night fell. The sky was cloudy and the air cool. Perla and Concha were fast asleep as I prepared for bed in the bedroom my sisters and I shared. As if from a distance, I heard Papá Apolonio call, "Luz Marina, why don't you, Mamá Sofía and I sit outdoors for a while, so we can talk."

"You are not home often these days," Mamá Sofía said, as I emerged from the room wearing my white *huipil*, the embroidery of many colours around the neckline.

The cooking fire in the hearth had burnt low. Overhead the sky had cleared and there was a full moon, bigger than I had ever seen. We sat together on a rough wooden bench set against the palmetto poles of our house.

"Such a fine man," Papá Apolonio said. "He likes and admires you so much, Luz Marina. He has asked my permission to become better acquainted with you."

Mamá Sofía was staring at the coals in the fire hearth which had burnt low. The fire crackled now and then and I could smell the wood smoke. It spiralled up towards the sky.

"I think he is thinking of asking you to marry him," Papá Apolonio said, rubbing his hands over the top of my head.

"It is as your Papá said, Luz Marina, a miracle from God."

"Two miracles," Papá Apolonio said, patting his legs. "The pain I hardly feel any more, and a fine marriage for our daughter."

The moon had gone, and the sky was cloudy again. They both put their arms around me, rocking me backwards and forwards as I wept and wept, putting my hands over my mouth to silence my cries.

The following afternoon we went to Dolores's home in order to attend the meeting of the Belize Environmental Action Group, which was to be held at another member's house.

"It is better for us to go," Mamá Sofía had said. "We'll just stay here, otherwise, getting more and more depressed."

As Tomás reversed the pick-up truck out of their yard, Dolores said, "That fire was outrageous. I am sorry you didn't come to us last night."

"We should have," Mamá Sofía said, "but they kept us a long time at the station. And we weren't thinking very straight, as you can imagine."

"I do believe one of the members could help you find a job, Luz Marina," Dolores said. "Mind you, it would probably be as a maid or something like that."

"I've been a maid before," I said, thinking of the years I worked at Doña Catalina's house. I wondered if Rufina would really send me a message. I doubted it very much. I began to accept the fact that it might be months, even years, before I saw my children again. They would have forgotten about me by then.

"Well, I'll mention it to a few people when we get there," Dolores said. "Your mother can always help me in the shop during the day. I like company."

"Gladly," Mamá Sofía said.

I was surprised when we turned into the driveway of a beautiful two-storeyed house on a hillside overlooking the town of San Joaquín. The windowpanes glittered in the late afternoon sunshine. The doors were open and people drifted in and out with drinks and plates of food.

"These are nice people," Dolores said. "And helpful too. Just be yourself." Tomás parked the pick-up truck and we started across the lawn.

Chairs were set out under giant, spreading trees and several dozen men and women moved about talking and laughing in small groups. Dolores and Tomás introduced Mamá Sofía and me to a few people and then she said, "Oh look, there's Carlos Ochoa Palmas. Let's go over and sit with him."

As we walked through the crowd of people gathered on the lawn, we came face to face with Elodio Alpuche Guerra, who smiled politely at us. We returned his smile. Mamá Sofía and I continued walking ahead, while Dolores and Tomás stopped to speak with Señor Elodio. Mamá Sofía and I hovered under a tree waiting for them.

"This is too bad, Luz Marina," Mamá Sofía said, a sympathetic expression in her eyes. She looked shyly towards where Señor Elodio stood, deep in conversation with Dolores and Tomás. Flowering shrubs and plants rimmed the perimeter of the house.

"Yes, Mamá Sofía, but what can we do?"

Except for Carlos Ochoa Palmas, we didn't really know anyone else at the meeting so we sat down on the chairs nearest to us. Eventually, Dolores and Tomás began walking in our direction. They were followed by Elodio Alpuche Guerra, a serious expression on his face, although his eyes looked at us with friendliness.

"I was congratulating Señor Elodio on joining the society," Dolores said to us.

"Thanks to Tomás's urging," Señor Elodio said. "A good turnout, eh, Tomás?"

"Yes," Tomás replied. "We are all looking forward to your presentation."

Mamá Sofía took a step towards Elodio Alpuche Guerra and said, "What are you going to talk about this evening, Señor?"

"Nothing very much, Señora. Tomás and Dolores have persuaded me to donate a few acres to the society." He paused and then said to us, "I am glad to see you both here."

He smiled, running his fingers through his hair. For a moment I glimpsed again the slim young boy I had known when we were both in San Joaquín Primary School. Dolores and Tomás were looking at me and I suddenly found myself saying, "Señor Ochoa has asked Mamá Sofía and me to do an interview about the newspaper article. I was wondering whether it is something we should do." I felt greatly relieved to be asking the advice of Elodio Alpuche Guerra.

"Why not? We are on the same side now, I think, doing what we can?" He looked at me gravely, with no hint in his eyes of the last day I had worked in his office.

"Perhaps you are right, Señor. It is something for me to think about. Please give my greetings to Rosa Christina and Pedro Fernandez."

"I will remember. Rosa Christina reminds me regularly that no one else files as carefully as you can."

Elodio Alpuche Guerra started to walk with Tomás to the speakers' table when he turned back and drew Mamá Sofía and me aside.

"I hope you will accept my apologies? Dolores and Tomás have talked things over with me. Doña Catalina left me with a different impression about your part in the matter. I am sincerely sorry."

"It is as nothing, Señor Elodio," I said, feeling my face go red. I smiled. Looking at him with amazement, Mamá Sofía said, "I am glad we are friends again, Señor."

Señor Elodio slipped his hands into the pockets of his trousers, and looked down at his shining brown shoes. "I think we must find a way to put the past behind us, Señora? I think your husband and my father would be glad."

"I agree, completely," Mamá Sofía said, her eyes far away.

As we sat down beside Carlos Ochoa Palmas, he smiled and said to me, "I don't suppose you've changed your mind about that interview?"

"Sometimes you need to speak out, Luz Marina," Dolores said, giving each of us a copy of the agenda.

Mamá Sofía said, "I'll do the interview if Luz Marina does."

My head was swimming as I looked at Elodio Alpuche Guerra seated with the other speakers at the long table covered with a white cloth. The euphoria of speaking with Señor Elodio had vanished. My throat felt constricted as I thought of Feliciano, Teresa and Eduardo.

"They'll take me to court," I said. "And I have my probation to think about."

"I won't ask for the names of any landowners," Carlos Ochoa said, "and I won't use your names, only your voices. Two people among many others I'll be using on this programme."

"All right," I said. Later, after the meeting ended, Mamá Sofía and I told Carlos Ochoa Palmas the little we knew. As we were being taped, I realised that Mamá Sofía and I were fighting for my children in the only way I could.

Dolores did find me a job with the family who owned the house where the meeting was held. It was an enormous house to clean, but I was glad to work hard. Mamá Sofía and I found a cheaper room to rent near Dolores's home, and we left the boarding house above Nora's Restaurant.

On the night our interview was on air, Dolores invited us to listen to Carlos Ochoa Palmas's radio programme in her shop. My voice, and Mamá Sofía's, were clear, but I was surprised to hear so many other voices talking about the sale of land in the area of San Joaquín.

"You see," Dolores said. "A lot of people are talking about it. The government will put a stop to it now, undoubtedly."

In the New Year Dolores allowed us to borrow her sewing machine. During the evenings Mamá Sofía and I began making costumes for sale during the next annual festival in honour of San Joaquín. As the weeks sped by we had given up hope of ever hearing from Rufina.

"Rufina and Ducho have their jobs to think about," Mamá Sofía said. "What would we do in their place, Luz Marina?"

One night, at the beginning of March, as we were cutting out a costume from a piece of yellow satin, Mamá Sofía said to me, "Resign yourself to the probation, Luz Marina. They might reduce it yet, who knows?"

"It's hard to accept, Mamá Sofía."

"I know. But think of the care they are getting, especially Feliciano."

"I can care for them, Mamá Sofía. And the members at Esperanza Evangelica would raise funds to help Feliciano, I feel sure."

"Papá Apolonio and I did the best we could at the time, Luz Marina. You are our daughter. We were concerned for your safety."

"I know, Mamá Sofía, I know," I said. I was cutting out the sleeves of the costume when the landlady knocked on the door. "Luz Marina, *teléfono*."

We hardly ever received telephone calls, especially at night. I immediately thought of Feliciano, and rushed down the hall, with Mamá Sofía hurrying behind me saying, "*Dios, Dios.*"

"Hello, this is Luz Marina," I said, my heart beating.

"Luz Marina, this is Rosa Christina. I am calling you from my house. How are you?"

"Fine, Rosa Christina, how are you?" I said, sitting down on the floor in relief. Mamá Sofía wiped the tears from her cheeks. We had been so frightened.

"Not fine at all, Luz Marina, to tell you the truth," Rosa said. "I'm having problems at Señor Elodio's office. You remember I told you about my baby? Well, it's due pretty soon and I want to work as late as possible. You know me – happy not to be at home!"

I smiled as I thought of Rosa's mother and her aunts.

Rosa continued, "Well, I'm getting so tired. Some mornings I get to work so late, and there's no help and the files are getting in disorder. I can't find anything. I said so to Señor Elodio just this morning, and do you know what he said to me, Luz Marina?"

"No, Rosa Christina."

"He said that I should call you to see if you are willing to come back and work with us. Where will they live, I asked him, and he said in your old rooms, of course! But you have a job, I suppose, Luz Marina?"

169

"Yes," I said. "I do some cleaning and light cooking."

"My God, and I need you at the office. The baskets are full, and the cabinets are in a mess. The salary at Señor Elodio's is much better, Luz Marina, and the accommodation and utilities are free. Can't you consider it?"

"Yes. Rosa Christina, oh yes. Mamá Sofía and I will be more than glad to return. But I need to give the family I work with two weeks' notice. They have been good to me."

"Two weeks, my God," Rosa Christina said. "Do what you need to do, Luz Marina, but come to us as soon as you can. I'll inform Señor Elodio in the morning. He'll be glad I solved our problem."

"I will, and thank you, Rosa, and my thanks to Señor Elodio."

I hung up the telephone, and hugged Mamá Sofía and we laughed and cried. "Life is large," Mamá Sofía said. "Just as Papá Apolonio always said. Such news! I'll write to Perla and Concha right away."

I gave two weeks' notice, as required, to the family in the house on the hill, and the days seemed to become so hopeful now, so full of purpose. After work one evening, shortly before festival week, I went as usual to Dolores's shop in the side street near the plaza. Mamá Sofía spent most of the day there until I returned. Then we walked back to our room together.

As I crossed the plaza near the fountain, I looked towards Doña Catalina's house, as I nearly always did, hoping for a glimpse of at least one of the children. I had not been lucky so far.

When I arrived at Dolores's shop, I was surprised to see Rufina waiting for me. She was sitting on a chair, while Dolores and Mamá Sofía attended to the customers. As soon as Rufina saw me at the door she hurried forward.

"Luz Marina, Doña Catalina wants you to visit her this evening about seven o'clock." She saw the fright on my face for she said, "Your children are all right and it might be a chance to see them, but I don't know."

It was hard to believe what she was saying. "Mamá Sofía," I called, "come and listen to this."

I knew I had to be careful. For several days in a row I had seen Ducho and Pescador near the fountain in the plaza. They had wanted me to see them, for Pescador had waved in a mocking way, and Ducho scowled at me before spitting on the ground. Like many people in San Joaquín, they believed the worst of me.

Rufina was repeating Doña Catalina's invitation to Mamá Sofía, who narrowed her eyes to slits as she looked into Rufina's face. "What are you saying, exactly, Rufina?"

"I swear to God, Señora Sofía. Why should I lie? I have a job to keep. I don't know what she wants."

"Did she say Luz Marina would see the children, Rufina?"

"No, Señora. Doña Catalina did not say anything like that."

Rufina bowed her head, and shrugged her shoulders, her eyes occasionally moving from Mamá Sofía's face to my own.

"Tell Doña Catalina I'll try to be there at seven, Rufina, and thanks for everything."

"*De nada, de nada*," she said, her face bleak. "So much is not the same."

After Rufina had disappeared down the street, Mamá Sofía and I told Dolores the entire situation and asked her advice. We talked about it for an hour, as Dolores and Mamá Sofía waited on the various customers who visited the shop.

In the end, Dolores said, "I don't see that you have too much choice. She may have decided to give you visiting rights. You never know. A change of heart is always possible."

"Maybe she heard our voices on the radio programme," I said.

"I'm sure she did, or somebody told her about it," Dolores said, "But it's still a free country as far as I know. And she is well aware of all you went through with Salvador."

"Luz Marina was devoted to Doña Catalina," Mamá Sofía said, "There was hardly a thing Luz wouldn't do for her."

They were silent for a moment but I knew they were thinking about Salvador, like I was. Whatever good things I had done had been undone in that one afternoon.

"You'll take your mother with you, of course," Dolores said, "That goes without saying."

At seven o'clock Mamá Sofía and I stood in the familiar portico and rang the bell. Rufina answered the door and we followed her past the parrot cages, filled now with ferns and other plants, up the wide, curving marble staircase, along the wide corridor and through the sitting room until we reached the *galería*.

I inhaled the scent of furniture polish and of leather. I listened for the voices of my children, but all was silent. The only lights on the *galería* were from the plaza and from the Church of San Joaquín.

Doña Catalina was seated in her usual chair, her face in shadow. Andrés lay sprawled on a cane sofa next to her, a drink in his hand. From the doorway I could smell her perfume, mixed with the scent of jasmine growing in giant clay jars at one end of the *galería*. It seemed as though we stood at the doorway for a long time before Doña Catalina said, "This is a business matter."

She did not ask us to step on to the *galería*, so we continued to stand in the doorway. My fingers touched the panels Don Higinio had carved all those years ago. I felt as Doña Catalina must feel: old, tired, heartbroken. I could not guess Mamá Sofía's thoughts. She gazed down at the tiled floor of the *galería*.

"Andrés and I discussed what you said on the radio programme. We feel it had very little basis in fact and indeed could be considered slander. However, we know that you must have been feeling very angry over the loss of your children. Perhaps you thought we were being greedy and unfair by not allowing you to see them. So, given the pressure you have been under, we are willing to forgive your actions."

"What do you say, Luz Marina?" Andrés's speech was slurred, his voice loud. "Do you think we have been greedy and unfair?"

"No," I said, "I do not think you have been unfair. You told me that Doña Catalina will do whatever is necessary to keep Feliciano, Teresa and Eduardo. You told me that she was willing to offer me a generous settlement."

"And what was your answer to that?" Andrés asked. I tried to remember that Andrés was Doña Catalina's one remaining child.

"I said no." I am sure they saw our faces clearly because the lights from the plaza shone directly on us.

"I also asked you very humbly, Luz Marina, never to speak about our affairs in public again. And you, Señora Figueroa, I am surprised at your actions, I must say."

I shrugged, and Mamá Sofía did not reply.

"Señora Figueroa," Andrés said, "didn't you and I try to do the best for your daughter?"

"I am not sure, Señor," Mamá Sofía replied. "It is difficult for me to remember."

Doña Catalina picked up her cane and laid it across her lap. "But we are willing to start again. I would like you both to leave the San Joaquín area as soon as possible."

Andrés sat up in the lounge chair and leaned towards us. "We've spent several days trying to placate business colleagues and government officials, as well as our foreign partners. Protests are being organised all over the country, even in England and the United States."

"This is not good for business," Doña Catalina said. "I am saddened that people seemed to have forgotten so quickly our contributions in San Joaquín, and your crime against our family."

"I have wanted to say how sorry I am, Doña Catalina, so very sorry. It was a terrible accident of that time. I am only asking for your understanding, not your forgiveness."

"Since you feel that way," Doña Catalina said, "the rest should not be difficult. I would also like to become the permanent guardian of my grandchildren."

"It is hard to refuse you, Doña Catalina, but I cannot do that. I returned to San Joaquín in the hope that you might allow me to see the children sometimes."

"I may be able to do that," Doña Catalina said, "on a regular basis but only after you have given them up to me."

"I cannot do that, Doña Catalina."

"Luz Marina," said Andrés, "my mother and I would like to buy you a house in the Bella Vista suburb in Belize City. It would be yours free and clear. We would also provide you with a thousand dollars per month for the rest of your life."

"And that money would be for giving up the children and leaving San Joaquín?" Mamá Sofía asked. Her eyes were angry, her voice strong, as she looked towards the figures whose faces we could not clearly see.

"And don't worry," Andrés added. "If our business affairs ever go to court, which is unlikely, we will make certain that you are able to spend those months in Mexico or Guatemala."

"The answer to everything is no, Doña Catalina," I said. "I will trust my affairs to the court."

"And to God," Mamá Sofía said.

"I must warn you both," Andrés said, getting up to stand against the railing of the *galeria*. "We have informed our business partners that we would try to reason with you. I will have to report that we failed."

"It is hard for me to believe," Doña Catalina said, her voice shaking, "that you are the person I brought into my home as a young woman."

"It is hard for me, too, Doña Catalina," I said, keeping my voice low, respectful, as I remembered that first day.

"We cannot be held responsible for the consequences," Doña Catalina said. She pressed a buzzer on the wall beside her. "Rufina will show you out."

As we walked with Rufina towards the door, I asked, "Where are the children, Rufina?"

"When I returned, Teresa and Eduardo had gone for a drive with Ducho. Poor Feliciano is asleep, and Doña Catalina would see me if I tried to take you into his room."

"Do they ask for me?"

"Often," Rufina said.

"What do you tell them?"

"The best I can, Luz Marina. I tell them that you had to go away and that you may not come back. Doña Catalina tells them the same."

Rufina closes the door quietly. Mamá Sofía and I stand on the portico for a minute. I want very badly to remain in the house that still feels like home to me, and where my children live. A strong March wind is blowing as we cross the plaza and I feel so cold.

Clear water tumbles down the several tiers of the fountain, spouting from the mouths of stone dolphins and other sea creatures, real and fantastical. Courting couples seem disguised by the rainbow colours of the arcing sprays splashing in the lighted fountain. They linger in its glow.

Parents sit on benches watching boys and girls run around the plaza, excited by the holiday lights and sparkling festival decorations.

Young people crowd around vendors selling peanuts, roasted pumpkin seeds and coconut sweets. Fruit sellers roll barrows, loaded with mangoes, oranges, grapefruit and watermelon, up and down the streets. Meat sizzles on charcoal fires.

Horns beep impatiently on the crowded streets, bicycle bells ring. It is nearing festival time again, and the doors of the Church of San Joaquín are open. People stream in and out of the church. Dozens of candles burn before a statue of the patron saint of our town.

"Let's go in," Mamá Sofía says. "Perhaps it will help to revive our spirits." I think we both want to remain as long as possible in the vicinity of Doña Catalina's home. Perhaps we are hoping that Doña Catalina will change her mind, that she will send Rufina to find us.

We sit in a front pew staring at the candles until they go out. As we walk back to our room, I say to Mamá Sofía, "Tomorrow, I will call the lawyer, Mr Reuben Oliver. I will tell him about my job at Señor Elodio's, with our old rooms on his *rancho*, and everything else that has happened. I will explain our situation. Who knows, maybe the court would consider my case, look at it with compassion."

"It's almost a year," Mamá Sofía replies. "We should at least try."

The next morning, before leaving for work, Mamá Sofía and I telephoned Mr Oliver, who was very receptive to the idea. He agreed to call or write to us within a week or so. It would be hard for us to wait.

On Saturday evening I walked through the plaza. I was on my way to deliver several costumes to a shopkeeper who had ordered them a few weeks before. I had now finished my job with the family on the hill, and Mamá Sofía and I were looking forward to Monday morning when I would start working in Elodio Alupuche Guerra's office, and we could move into the rooms on his *rancho*.

We had decided that I would continue sewing at night, and Mamá Sofía would start baking again. In this way we would earn extra money to furnish the Elodio Alupuche Guerra rooms with at least a few of the things to which my children had become accustomed in Doña Catalina's home. We still had a few days to wait before we could expect a call from Mr Reuben Oliver.

"A small fridge, I think," Mamá Sofía had said, adding up the figures on a piece of paper.

"And beds, don't forget," I had said, thinking about sheets, mosquito netting, and a crib large enough for Feliciano.

We were hoping that if Mamá Sofía and I had a suitable place for the children, the court would agree to let me have them. I felt certain we could accomplish these necessary things by the time I went before the judge again.

On Avenue Cahal Pech, where Doña Catalina's house is located, I looked up at the *galeria* but it was dark. I wondered if she was sitting in her chair watching me pass by. The streets were crowded and noisy. At the crossroads, I had to wait. A religious procession was slowly making its way to the Church of San Joaquín. The marchers carried candles shielded by paper cups, crosses and a statue of San Joaquín, bright paper garlands around the neck. The air was thick with incense. A brass band played a solemn hymn and people were singing.

Keeping its distance from the procession was a small band of drunken revellers, dancing to guitar music. They wore black costumes and, over their faces, heads and shoulders, headdresses that were intricately contrived to look like the heads and necks of birds. They were drawing a sizeable crowd and I couldn't help but pause to watch. I saw toucans, macaw parrots, white hawks, king vultures and owls. People clapped enthusiastically.

After the revellers had passed, I dashed across the street. Someone called my name, and I stopped, surprised. Two men, in costumes and masks, came up to me. I could smell the liquor on their breaths. My heart started to race for it was easy to recognise Ducho, who was smaller than most people. I also recognised Pescador's voice.

"Let's go for a walk, Luz Marina."

"No!" I shouted, again and again, but I knew immediately that the brass band at the door of the church was drowning out my protests. Pescador repeated, "Let's go." His grip on my elbow was so painful that the package of costumes I had carefully ironed fell from my arms into the dirty drain water.

I did not fight as they pushed me through crowds of costumed people singing and dancing. Groups of musicians seemed to be playing everywhere. I looked frantically around trying to catch someone's attention but, in San Joaquín, two men escorting a woman along the street is not a very unusual sight, particularly on a festival night.

We reached a back street I did not recognise and it was absolutely deserted. Pescador was saying to me, "Why don't you leave San Joaquín like a good girl? Nobody wants you here." He pushed me against a cement wall, slapping my face from side to side. As he turned around to see what Ducho was doing, I pulled away, picked up an empty pint bottle from the drain, and smashed it against the wall. The jagged ends glinted. I pressed my back against the wall as they approached, prepared to defend myself against their attack.

Ducho said softly, "Oho, the killer-woman, Xtabai. So this is how you murdered Salvador Joaquín. You sneaked up on him early one morning while he was asleep and you cut open his neck. Everyone knows that's how you did it."

"No!" I shouted. "No!"

"Yes," Ducho said.

They bent down and picked up stones from the street. One by one, they threw them at me, aiming for my face and head. Each time I shouted, "No!" Ducho or Pescador shouted "Yes!" louder and louder. One stone hit my temple. I found myself sitting in the drain, the broken bottle in my hand.

I was getting tired and weak and the pain in my head was almost unbearable. Crouched in the drain, feeling the stones pelting me and hearing the voices of Ducho and Pescador, I remembered the afternoon Salvador pulled me naked out of the bathhouse by my hair. I had tried not to scream. Teresa and Eduardo were playing nearby. Feliciano was in his crib, and Concha had gone with Mamá Sofía and Papá Apolonio to a neighbour's house.

Salvador slapped my face over and over again. He twisted my hair around and around so that I thought he would pull my hair out of my scalp. As he raised his right leg in a kick, his grip loosened and I staggered back, falling to the concrete floor of the open bathhouse. Scrambling to my knees, I tried to close the door against Salvador. I heard Teresa and Eduardo crying, "Don't hurt Mamá, don't hurt Mamá." Salvador wrenched the door from my grasp. Pain, rage and helplessness engulfed me. Crouched in a corner, I felt the handle of Papá Apolonio's machete digging into my shoulders. Salvador, his drunken breath on my face, had put his hands around my throat and he was squeezing, squeezing.

I grasped Papá Apolonio's machete with my right hand and I swung it at Salvador's head with a strength I did not know I possessed. At first I felt nothing but sweet relief, release, my chest heaving as I gasped for air. I opened my eyes and saw Salvador beside me, blood pouring from a gaping wound in his neck. I couldn't believe it. I wouldn't believe it, but after a while I realised that he was no longer breathing. People in San Joaquín say that grief is a monster with many faces. Now I knew the truth of this belief. My teeth were chattering loudly and I was shivering with cold. I stuffed my fist into my mouth to prevent myself from screaming. How could I have done this to Salvador? It was too much to think about.

After a while, I don't know how long, I found myself in the bedroom of my parents' house. I wrapped a sheet around my body and sat on the floor, my head leaning against Feliciano's crib. Teresa and Eduardo sat beside me, screaming. They implored me to get up and to help their Papá Salvador.

In my mind, I saw Mamá Sofía and Papá Apolonio staring at us in horror. Concha sponged the blood from my body and helped me to dress. I remembered walking away with Teresa and Eduardo to the Church of San Joaquín. I thought of Papá Apolonio's machete which he always sharpened on both sides. I had not intended to kill Salvador, but the machete had found its mark.

Pescador and Ducho continued stoning me with ever larger pieces of rock. As they drew nearer, I raised the bottle and caught sight of the glinting edges. I heard the prison guard saying, "Once a killer, a killer twice. We'll have the new prison ready by the time you return." I thought of Feliciano, Teresa and Eduardo. I flung the bottle across the street and heard it crash and splinter.

As Ducho and Pescador rushed towards me, there was a sudden burst of music and singing voices not too far away. "This is for Salvador Joaquín," Pescador said as they pounded my head with their fists. "Let's go, Pesca," Ducho said. "People are coming." The pain in my head was very bad. I leaned my head against the wall, waiting for strength.

For a while I thought I was in Salvador's house by the river, and as he hit my jaw with his fist I said, "No more, please,

Salvador, no more." I heard guitar music. Salvador and I were dancing, and the children were clapping. Salvador's voice was rich and sweet, as he sang, "The girl that I love is a little brown girl because she dances *la bamba*." It felt so good to lay my head against his heart and rest ...

Mamá Sofía, Dolores and the police did not find me until a long time after midnight. Someone in the marching band had telephoned the police station. I was in the San Joaquín Hospital for many weeks. Sometimes there when I woke from a dream, or a nightmare, Mamá Sofía and Dolores were sitting close to my bed.

On one of those days, I was in considerable pain, and longing for the nurse to give me my medication so I could fall asleep. Mamá Sofía seemed to be saying, "Luz Marina, Rufina told the police that she heard Ducho and Pescador joking about a plan to accost and beat you in the plaza, but she never believed they would do it."

"Poor Rufina," I said, but I was not sure Mamá Sofía and Dolores always heard me when I spoke. In my mind I could hear Don Pablo's booming laugh, "Too, too incredible," he was saying to Rufina. The parrots were strangely quiet and I wondered about that. So I went down the marble staircase to see if something was the matter with them.

But when I opened my eyes, a nurse had drawn the curtain around my bed. I felt the prick of the needle, but it was as nothing compared with the pain in my mind and heart. The doctor visited me each day. I resolved to tell her that I now remembered, and could never forget, the very instant I used Papá Apolonio's machete to take the life of Salvador Joaquín. May God have mercy on his soul, and on my own. The clarity, the brightness, of that certain, terrible moment in memory, pierced my eyes. They ached, and I longed for unending sleep.

On some other day, Mamá Sofía came to see me much earlier than usual. I closed my eyes against the light flooding through the open windows. Mamá Sofía shook my shoulders gently and I tried to look at her but the bright sunshine hurt my eyes.

The medication made me sleep a lot, for which I was grateful. I did not want to think or do anything very much. I wished I could just lie in the bed in this hospital ward for ever. It seemed like a safe place; here I had no responsibilities. I now dreaded the day I would have to leave.

"Hello, Mamá Sofía," I said, but I was not sure she heard my voice.

"It's too early for a long visit, Luz Marina," Mamá Sofía was saying, "but the nurse said I could see you for one minute. Try to pay attention, *corazón*."

She put my hand against her cheek; it was wet. I was sorry my Mamá Sofía was crying. I didn't want her to cry and be sad. I myself was tired of crying. I wished to smile at my Mamá Sofía, but it was difficult.

"A court date has been set, Luz Marina. Mr Oliver has asked many people to testify on your behalf. The pastor of Evangelica is going to Belize City, so is Dolores, and Señor Elodio. The doctor will be there, I believe, and your probation officer."

I stared at Mamá Sofía in total incomprehension. I had dreams and nightmares quite often so at this moment I was not sure I understood her words. I tried to sit up, but my head ached so I lay back against the pillows.

"Dolores and Tomás believe you will get custody of your children now. I wanted to tell you immediately!"

Mamá Sofía seemed to slip in and out of the light. I tried to focus on her eyes, on the wrinkles in her face, on the hope in her voice, but it was too much. Really.

Mamá Sofía poured water into a basin on the night table, and wiped my face gently with a wet rag. "Your children will need you. Pluck up your courage, Luz Marina. Try to be well, Luz Marina."

I tried to smile at my Mamá Sofía but I wanted to go to sleep again. Perhaps I would dream of the river in the icy cold caves in the mountains which Salvador told me about. In San Joaquín we believe spirits live in those caves; perhaps Salvador would be there. But who knows? Like Don Pablo, Salvador could be anywhere, and I couldn't tell when he would return home.

"Expect me at any time, Luz Marina," Salvador used to say.

"How are you feeling?" Mamá Sofía asked, starting to wipe my arms, examining the scars. "They are healing up nicely," she said.

I opened my eyes, unsure of the day and the time. I felt a little surprised to see the hospital ward for I had been dreaming of Salvador's house by the river. The children were at the dining table shouting with laughter. Their happy voices mingled with the rushing sounds of the river outside the kitchen door.

"Tell us that joke again, Papá Salvador," they were urging him.

"Tell us the one about the rabbit, Papá," Teresa said.

"And remember to wiggle your ears," Feliciano added.

"One ear or two?" Salvador asked, looking into Eduardo's giggling face. And little Eduardo, so sweet, really, he held up two small fingers and Salvador cried, "Bravo, Eduardo," and Teresa and Feliciano clapped their hands, and Salvador looked so proud.

"Can you hear me, Luz Marina?" Mamá Sofía was saying. She seemed to be bending very close to my face. "How are you feeling today?"

"Not very good, Mamá Sofía." I closed my eyes. A drowsiness was coming over me and I was so very glad.

The noise in the hospital ward woke me up late one afternoon. It was visiting time and Mamá Sofía sat at my bedside. "Good news, Luz Marina, such good news, can you hear me?"

I nodded, looking at the excitement in her eyes.

"Mr Reuben Oliver is here, Luz Marina. He wants to talk with you."

I looked towards the door of the ward and saw Mr Oliver. He walked to my bed and sat down on a chair. Looking at his cheerful face and bright smile, it was hard for me to believe that Mr Oliver was in San Joaquín. I remembered the day I said goodbye to him at the bus station on Mosul Street in Belize City, so long ago it seemed now.

Mamá Sofía was holding both my hands. She pressed them against her mouth, her breath warm against my skin. The noise in the ward was very great. Mr Oliver drew the curtain around the bed. I sat up against the pillows and pushed my hair away from my face, surprised to feel how much it had grown. I tried to smile at Mr Oliver and he said, "The court has no objection if your children rejoin you, Luz Marina."

I continued to smile as I listened to Mr Oliver. It is my experience that things, like words, are often not what they seem to be.

"However," he said, "you will still be under probation for the remaining two years."

I looked at my Mamá Sofía who was crying and nodding.

"In addition," Mr Oliver was saying, "you need to continue seeing Dr Douglas, Mrs Wade, your probation officer, and other court appointed officers."

Mr Oliver looked very pleased and so proud. "You will continue your community work with the pastor, of course."

Mr Oliver was such a polite man, and so very kind. I thought of my last day in the Belize City Supreme Court. In my mind, I saw the rectangular dock, made of dark mahogany, glowing in the sunshine. I saw Mr Oliver standing below the judge's seat, high above him. I heard the judge's voice above the rustle of papers, and the clearing of throats in the courtroom.

"During this period, your doctor will continue to evaluate your progress."

The judge must have recently repeated these words to Mr Oliver, I felt sure. But he knew that I had heard them before and that I understood. So I said, "Thank you, Mr Oliver. But in what manner will my children rejoin me?" I thought of Doña Catalina and felt sure she would never give them up. Mamá Sofía's face was in her hands and her shoulders were shaking. I could not tell whether she was crying from happiness, or from grief.

Mr Oliver stood up and pulled the curtain back from the bed. I heard the rings rattle against the curved metal rod.

"I didn't want to startle you," Mr Oliver said, "but the Casals are under a court order. Two of your children are here to visit you. Feliciano is in Elodio Alpuche Guerra's home until you are able to return there."

"Perla!" Mamá Sofía was calling softly as she hurried away to the door of the ward, which seemed a long distance away. "Perla!"

"Steady now," Mr Reuben Oliver is saying to me, but my legs are already over the side of the bed, and I am trying to find my slippers. I must look so strange with two colours in my hair. Ay, *Dios*.

I am so happy, so weak, perhaps it is true.

"You look fine," Mr Oliver is saying to me. "Never better, except for the fact that you are not smiling, Luz Marina."

"No, no," I say, tears rolling down my face. "I can't think about smiling at a time like this. I am too nervous." My fingers are icy cold. I feel so much like I did on the days before I entered the courtroom in Belize City.

"I have never known you to be too nervous to smile," Mr Oliver says, and as I concentrate on the doorway, I smile.

"You are right, Mr Oliver," I reply, as I used to say on court days.

I see Perla and Mamá Sofía at the door kneeling beside Teresa and Eduardo. Perla is showing them where I am. I hold out my arms to Teresa and Eduardo, thinking that soon I will see Feliciano again.

"Mamacita!" Teresa is shouting. "Mamacita!" She is dragging Eduardo along and she is saying to him, "It's Mamá, Eduardo, Mamá. Can't you see?"

"*Si?*" Eduardo is asking, I feel sure, for as he glances around the ward, his little face looks doubtful.

"Yes, Eduardo, yes," Teresa must be saying, for as they draw nearer, I suddenly hear Eduardo shout, exultation in his voice, "Mamá, Mamá, we are here!"

Indeed. My face is buried in Teresa's silky black curls and my hand presses Eduardo against me, hearing him ask, "Why did you go away, Mamá, why?"

I feel so much relief, such sweet release. I hold them away from me and see Salvador in Teresa's deep-set dark eyes, and in Eduardo who is smiling, his lips curving upwards like Salvador's used to do. I think of Feliciano in his crib at the Elodio Alpuche Guerra *rancho*. Feliciano's hair is thick and black, and grows away from his forehead like Salvador's used to do.

I have no answers ready yet for my children, so I am silent. In Teresa's eyes is a look of devastation which I realise must be in my own.

But I am bound and determined to be well again, to be as good a mamá as my own Mamá Sofía. I am trying not to think of the sad and terrible burden my children and I will need to bear. At this moment, I seem to feel the spirit of the Salvador we loved rising to meet our own. Perhaps he would have said impatiently, "Forget about it, Luz Marina. It is not important now!"

Each year, God willing, in repentance, and in thanksgiving, I will offer up a special mass during the Festival of San Joaquín. I will wear a black mantilla over my hair, and candlelight will fill my eyes.

The Macmillan Caribbean Writers Series

Series Editor: Jonathan Morley

Look out for other exciting titles from the region:

Crime thrillers:

Fiction:

Short Stories:

Poetry:

Plays: